SALV
DIVING FOR

DOMINIC L. MILLER

Contents

Acknowledgements

01. Return to Newhaven 1
02. Shore Break 10
03. Full English 20
04. River of Strife 30
05. Far Flung Finances 38
06. Dangerous Drift 46
07. Partner Poser 55
08. Bicycle Basin 64
09. Going Dutch 73
10. The Navy Tot 82
11. Showroom to Scotland 90
12. Wee Four 101
13. Good Ship *Galloper* 110
14. Press down 119
15. Dive Number One 128
16. Bar Hatch 138
17. Bubble Trouble 146
18. Revolt 155
19. Dive Number Six 163
20. Bar #28 171
21. Framework 179
22. Decompression 187
23. Peterhead Plunge 195
24. Golden Hour 203
Epilogue 213

Copyright

© 2022 by Dominic L Miller

All rights reserved. No part of this book may be reproduced or used in any manner without the express written permission of the publisher, except for the use of brief quotations in a book review. Sorry, has to be said.

ISBN: 9798353191506

Imprint: Independently published

Edited by Hugh Barker

Cover art and design © by Dominic Forbes

IN MEMORY OF GEORGES ARNOUX

Based on true events & inspired by others

Having said that...

All characters and events featuring in this work are fictitious. Any resemblance to real persons, dead or alive, or events, is purely coincidental.

And lastly, please ensure to register all subsea finds with the Receiver of Wreck, or your local equivalent.

Acknowledgements

This is my way of honouring the courageous breed known as "Pioneer Divers", of which I count my Uncle Brian as one, and ensuring their stories of bravery or otherwise are not lost to me, you and everyone else. Put simply, it is a profession where your first mistake may very well be your last. My task as the writer thereafter, if I may call myself that, is to aim to work as many of these as is possible into an enjoyable, plausible and coherent plot that has a beginning, an end and some interesting stuff between.

Since publishing Salvamar in 2019, I have made contact with various former colleagues, peers and associates of my Uncle Brian. In particular, a number are worth a special mention here for their constant support and encouragement. Gordon Clark is the owner of an amazing brain, and a fountain of diving knowledge on legs. Martin Woodward M.B.E. shared fond memories of working with my uncle and is still diving today and unearthing many a lost shipwreck in the Solent waters around his Isle of Wight home. Tom Wingen, who resides in Norway, was the first ex-colleague of Uncle Brian I encountered after Salvamar was published. He is a straight-talking Canadian who has revealed many of his exploits throughout our conversations. Since we met in August 2020 in Plymouth, Ray Ives provided many pictures of himself working in various parts of the world – each with written recollections explaining the image on the rear. All of them are responsible for supplying me with true stories, textured with great detail.

The many drafts of Salvamar II were written between November 2021 to September 2022 in the following places – Cadaques in Spain, Brugges in Belgium and Cape Town in South Africa, but don't tell my girlfriend as I was meant to be on holiday. Final read-through tweaks and polishing were performed in Issirac, France. For all the exotica associated with these locations, the bulk of the writing was completed in Haarlem in the Netherlands.

A huge thank you to my partner – Lina. The funny, beautiful lady who puts up with me and has yet to perform a midnight flit, fleeing me and our relationship in the process.

I hope you enjoy the next Salvamar instalment.

Dominic

Amsterdam - 2022

01. Return to Newhaven

"Is that you, Bri?" Bill asked optimistically.

He was on his knees and bracing himself with his hands in the stubby bow of their dinghy. Bill had watched the eerie jade orb of light, with Brian at its core, emerge up the buoy line from the otherwise black depths of the Channel. The 40 minutes of topside duties for Brian, alone on an inflatable skiff during the early hours of the morning in a treacherous shipping lane, had worked on Bill's nerves somewhat. With just a spare scuba mask, compass and map as company, any one of those fraught minutes could have seen a sudden change of wind or current for the worse. Battling seasickness and with towering tankers passing by close enough to feel the vibrations of their engines, Bill's appetite for Brian's type of adventure was waning as soon as it had started.

The rain showers passing overhead had saturated his grey ski-jacket. Before leaving for Newhaven Bill had grabbed the tight hood for his son's coat, so it fitted more like a sheer swimming cap. The gales had done little to dry his clothing.

"Yep. I'm over here," Brian shouted inside his helmet, swimming towards their boat and breathing heavily. He lifted himself up over the side of the dinghy, hooked his elbows over the far side of the inflated rib and asked for assistance from his dive support. The knuckle of his thumb opened the locking mechanism to seal the helmet to his neck scarf.

"Help me get this stuff up, Bill. I can't feel my *baastard* hands."

"Righto, Bri."

Crawling on his hands and knees, Bill waited for Brian to slowly remove and hand up his flippers and three spent tanks of air.

"God, I forgot how cold it is down there. Right, I'm next. Grab a handful of the back of my suit and lift up when I climb in. Ready? 1, 2, 3, lift!"

Bill landed Brian next to him on the V-shaped floor of the dinghy. Water poured off his waterlogged dry suit as Brian turned over to sit up and start scanning the immediate horizon. He told Bill about an encounter with a sea creature as he shifted himself into position; his cumbersome limbs were heavy without the effect of weightlessness. "I think I had a tope after me down, ahh, there."

"What's a tope, Bri?"

"Like a British shark I suppose, ahh. About six foot long, ahh. I saw its tail a few, ahh, times in the light from my torch on my way back up. Ahhhh!"

"Ch...rist, Bri."

"Right. Did you see anything come up by the boat?"

"No, Bri. I've been shitting bricks up here waiting though. I think I'd rather come down there with you than bloody wait up here," Bill said as he nervously corrected imbalances created in the craft by Brian first arranging himself, then making his way to the stern to get the outboard motor started.

"I had to come up slow, so I was about five minutes behind it. You didn't hear anything either? Like a big splash?"

"No. Not a sausage, Bri."

"Right, we'll have to find the *baastard* then. It can't be far," Brian said just before yanking the pull-cord. The 10 horsepower engine sparked into life reassuringly. Before releasing their rope around the buoy marking the wreck beneath, he leant forward to grab the torch. He switched it on and shone it at Bill. He looked terrified; his eyes were on stalks and mouth aghast as he looked at his crazy friend. The direction the boat was pointing indicated the weak, but ever-strengthening current. "OK, we're pointing this way, so it should be floating behind us somewhere. Take the torch while I drive."

"What's floating behind us, Bri?"

"A safe. Hanging under two white lift bags."

"No really? You mean, like treasure?"

In some kind of triumph over the realisation his hunch may have proved right, Brian's lower jaw extended before a smile broke across it. "Yeah, I fucking hope so." The throttle handle turned in Brian's palm and the search began, working in ever-increasing loops away from the

Dalhousie wreck site. Brian's trepidation grew during the first two rounds, but settled on the disorientating third as he caught sight of the bulbous, cubed surface of one of the lift-bags.

"Magic! Pass that rope Bill. Right, can you come this end to keep her steady for a bit?"

As soon as the rope was in Brian's hand, he leapt back over the side of the dinghy into the inky swell.

"Bloody hell, Bri. What are you doing now?" Bill asked in an ascending pitch while moving across the dinghy, but Captain Worley clearly didn't hear him.

The lift bags hung rigidly in the water, their salvaged jetsam swaying below. Brian sucked in a huge breath and pulled himself underneath, aiming for the shackle connecting the bags to a rope lashed around the Victorian booty. Using a skill he had honed working in darkness on ocean floors around the world, with eyes as good as blindfolded and hands again paralysed by the cold, he tied the tow-rope through the rings that unified each of the wide webbing load-points surrounding the bags.

Brian's second return onto their craft was no more elegant than the first and Bill nearly went overboard himself when he lost grip of the back of the dry suit mid-heave. Like a silent whistle, Brian blew a series of forceful breaths through his lips, clearing away bitter seawater that drained down from his hair, before assuming control of the helm and giving his crew member the good news.

"Right Bill, get the compass out. We can go home now."

"Aye aye Bri. I left it where I was sitting earlier."

"We'll have to take it slow, mind. We're pulling a lot of weight behind us now."

"OK, Bri."

Through better judgement or blind fortune, Bill didn't ask what would be the outcome if the lift bags deflated or detached themselves from the hanging safe during their return passage, as the probable answer was they would be dragged down with it. At roughly the equivalent speed of a carnival float, four or five knots (six with an agreeable wind) Bill advised Captain Worley of the correct heading through the fumbled use of a compass, torch and the sopping map which was slowly converting itself to paper maché en route. He gave occasional glances to the horizon through the intermittent drizzle. The wintry sky was still too dark to provide any warning of the next shower.

"No. Not yet, bit more left. Yeah, north-north-west it is, now just aim us portside of the left lighthouse when we can see it better, Bri. That one's Beachy Head pal," Navigator Hicks said. They were using the same landmark to navigate back to Newhaven that had featured in reports of the sinking of the ship from which Brian had just raised the safe. It had always been a prominent landmark for shipping on the southern Sussex coast of England.

"Magic, Bill. Cheers."

Their progress was now more akin to a relaxing river cruise, with the nearest land having been a good ten miles off their bow when they started back.

"This is going to take hours. We got enough petrol haven't we, Bri?"

Captain Worley assessed the fuel supplies by lifting the oily plastic can under his bench seat and shook the frothy contents.

"Yeah, we should be OK," Brian said optimistically, not wanting to inflict any more fear upon his crew. Bill had been a willing partner in many of their former escapades, but, from the expression Brian had last seen in the beam of the torch, he had never been so scared. Now Bill reacted to a sharp cloudburst that felt like jabbing pins on his exposed hands and unsealed neck with a question that reinforced this point.

"Oh god, you haven't got another of those dry suits have you? Ch... rist! Mind you, if I was wearing one, it would be full of shit up to my knees by now!"

"Mine already is," Brian joked with watery eyes.

Whenever the rain from above did peter out, the chaotic spray from the sea could be relied upon to take over. Bill could not have been wetter standing in his shower.

Conversation was scarce before they began to feel the anger of the Channel fade closer into shore. Bill ensured they maintained their course. Brian was constantly casting an eye over his haul past the stern, in the creamy lather of their wake. The understandable tension associated with retrieving and bringing the safe back to shore gave way to feelings of confidence that they would manage to complete their task against significant odds. The twinkling onshore lights had expanded in size, lifting their spirits; the first squawking gulls and a welcoming series of flashing cardinal buoys marked the correct route back into Newhaven. Bill asked a few questions Brian should have known the answer to, but Brian's "work it out when you get there" approach to life had never been more prevalent than that morning.

"So what's in the safe, Bri?"

"Silver bars, I hope. But I've only felt them."

"So how do we get it onto land? You'll need a crane or something, won't you?"

"Yeah bloody right, Bill."

"Have you got one?"

"No. But better to bring it up than leave the *baastard* out there."

"Bloody hell, Bri."

"We still have to get there yet. We may have one more problem before that."

"What d'you mean, Bri?"

"You know the I.R.A. tried to top Thatcher a couple of months back with that bomb? I've read there are extra police patrols around at the moment, so keep 'em peeled!" Bill knew exactly what Brian was referring to; they had driven past the Grand Hotel on the seafront in Brighton on their way to Newhaven and seen the hasty repairs already being carried out to the central portion of the building, which had collapsed in the blast.

"Shit Bri." Reading Brian's hesitance at this prospect, Bill asked, "I'm guessing we shouldn't be towing the safe behind us?"

"No, we shouldn't. Not without declaring it to the Receiver of Wreck."

"Oh bollocks. You didn't tell me that, Bri."

"Don't worry, Bill. We'll be fine," Brian said. "There won't be many boats out at this time."

Minute fissures in the clouds allowed for subtle improvements in the amount of daylight on offer. Glimpses of each other were increasingly possible without a torch. Wide-eyed Bill in his soaked grey jacket, nylon bonnet and jeans. Brian wisely still zipped up in his cherry red dry suit with tight rubberised seals formed on his wrist and neck cuffs. A scuba mask was pushed up to his browline, where it had stayed after connecting the tow rope. Now he wore an uncharacteristic scowl. A fragile, triumphant peace lasted but a few minutes in Brian's mind before spotting something unwelcome in the distance.

"Oh shit," Brian said, breaking their silence. "That boat is coming towards us isn't it?" A faint blue light started flashing on the boat in question, in time with the conclusion of Brian's question. Bill's reply wasn't required. "*Baastard*. We don't have a radio so they'll be coming alongside us. How long until they reach us, Bill?"

"They're going a fair lick, Bri. Couple of minutes max?" Bill estimated nervously, watching the gap narrowing all the while.

With little time left and even less to contemplate, Brian released the twist throttle then pulled the scuba mask wedged against his forehead back down over his eyes. "Oh fuck. Pass that knife, Bill." He slid his left hand down the tow rope, held his grip there and, in a single motion, swung himself up out of the dinghy like a Fosbury flop, back into the sea.

02. Shore Break

"Hurry up, Bri!"

Brian was sightlessly clawing away seaweed that had collected during the return and hacking his way through the rope secured around the corroded safe. With his own weight applied to the load, he kept the lift-bags below the surface as much as possible once they were free of the ill-gotten load. Led only by the frequency of the serrations drawing through the strands of the rope, he judged one or two cuts remained to drop the safe, so sucked in a last breath while checking the dimly lit surrounds for a bearing. The silhouette of the fort, an imposing fortification built during WW2 capped the bluff overlooking the arcing concrete breakwater, which marked the western spout of the port at its rounded end.

"How far off the end of that breakwater are we Bill? Roughly?" Brian requested of his navigator, his own perspective restricted to the surface as he took another chest full of air.

"200 feet. 150 feet, something like that."

"Right. And the marker buoy, the nearest one?"

"About 150 feet the opposite direction, Bri."

Brian asked his last question when he already knew the answer. "How long until the police reach us?"

"Shit, not long. A minute? Their siren's going now, Bri."

"Right, I won't be long." Brian could hear it too.

Under Bill's guidance, they had been following the main passage into the harbour, and so were above its deepest portion. Three rather fevered slices through the final taut fibres were needed to separate the safe, after which it plunged to the base of the deep shipping channel, hopefully far enough below the draft of the largest ferry or tanker. Brian immediately stabbed the woven nylon sides of both lift-bags to deflate them, releasing great gushes of bubbling air until their resistance in the water became limp. Rather than incriminating them, the presence of the lifting apparatus in the dinghy, on top of the spent scuba tanks, would provide their best hope of a cover story.

With patrols heightened and few other targets daft enough to set out to sea on that inhospitable December dawn, the not unsuspicious shipmate scoundrels readied themselves for an inspection and probable questioning. Bill unsteadily helped pull the empty bags aboard and Brian had just settled himself back beside the idling motor when the spotlight hit them. Squinting in the glare behind an open palm casting shade, Brian removed the mask from his forehead and tossed it slowly onto the floor, before seeking Bill's permission.

"Do you want me to do the bullshitting, Bill?"

"Bloody right, boy!"

Brian lightly increased the revs to move away from where he had dumped the safe, in the direction of the patrol boat, an action he hoped suggested willingness to comply and, more importantly, innocence. Just two wandering mariners simply enjoying some recreational time upon the water, with the means to plunder shipwrecks as cargo.

Below the searchlight, two figures were visible in the confined, white cabin on the police launch. They were behind a pair of fogged up windows and a squeaky door at the rear, facing the small open stern. A faded orange band ran the length of the weathered blue hull, just above the waterline. It was roughly 30 feet in length, thrice that of Brian and Bill's rib dinghy. The boats glided towards one another until they were close enough and both engines sounded a momentary reverse grumble to arrest their movement. Brian gripped the solid side of the police cabin cruiser, with the two opposing hulls bouncing off each other as the cabin door opened. An officer emerged, pulling down his diced banded service cap. A few lines of a Status Quo song escaped the cabin before the door was swiftly pulled shut by his colleague. He looked down at the pair of floating rascals, one bearded and grinning, the other dishevelled and quivering – Brian could probably have claimed he had found Bill lost out in the Channel, clinging to a section of flotsam.

"Good morning gents?" Brian and Bill both returned the greeting, fearful of what was to follow. "We were unable to contact you by radio, so we had to come and challenge you having watched you on our radar screen for the last while. I'm Officer Gradwell, I'm sure I don't need to show you my police badge, do I?"

"No that's fine. We believe you."

"I would just like to ask you a few questions, then you can be on your way."

"Be my guest," Brian returned with confidence.

Bill refrained from offering any responses, verbal or physical, so the officer's scrutiny was aimed increasingly at Captain Worley.

"Right, can I have some names please?"

"Ryan Worley and Phil Hicks," Brian claimed fraudulently. It was a habit he had when providing information to the police: a change of name close enough that could be passed off as having been misheard.

"OK and do you both live in the area, gents?"

"I do, officer. In Brighton, Phil lives in Essex."

"Do you mind explaining what you're both doing out here at seven o'clock on such a horrible morning?"

"Just some night shore-diving, but we've given up." That explained the tanks of compressed air by Brian's feet and the dry suit he sat in. The only flaw in this statement was the appearance of his fellow "diving enthusiast" Bill, in his tennis shoes, drenched denims and sopping ski jacket.

"What were you doing in the water? We observed you getting back onto your dinghy when we first shone our light on you both."

Pointing at the punctured lift bags partially covering the scuba tanks, Brian claimed "these *baastard* things got jammed around my prop as we were coming back in, so I had to cut them free." This slightly brazen yet completely unverifiable account preceded a lengthy silence from the officer, allowing him to both scratch his forelock and survey the cargo supporting their alibi. As they didn't appear to be members of the Irish Republican Army or have an outboard engine strong enough to venture much further out, they felt his interest wane as they were waiting for his response. The questioning officer was well aware that every time they cast off for another day of patrolling, they were entering the lawless no-man's-land on the water, precisely the reason Brian was so drawn to the high seas – or to working underneath them.

"Alright guys. I won't delay you any longer, thanks for your time. Make sure you behave yourselves on the way in," the officer said, with a knowing wink.

"Magic. We will."

They remained in place as they watched the launch continue their patrol until it was at a safe distance, then their stifled giggles finally erupted.

"Jesus Christ, Bri. That was close," Bill managed while exhaling loudly. "Can we bloody go home now?"

"How did we get away with that? Bullshit baffles brains, they say," a wide-eyed Brian replied with an incredulous smirk before turning his view back to the land they would be back on soon. "Right. Let's go home, Bill."

Their heads continued to shake in disbelief during the final stretch of their adventure. Now off mute, Bill was wanting to know why they had had to dump the safe. It had all happened so quickly that he had not questioned what Brian was up to, he just assisted like the fine friend he was. And he also wanted to know why Brian was not displaying the slightest trace of disappointment; if anything, he had seemed to revel in their unfinished escapade. This was in spite of the fact he had potentially been risking his life by diving to retrieve the treasure. In Bill's eyes, their jaunt out to the wreck site in the dead of night, regardless how insane it was, had proved unfruitful due to their encounter with the police. By contrast, Brian saw a corroded safe full of silver (at the very least) at the base of a shipping channel – sheltered from getting snagged in fishing nets and discovery by other recreational divers. The only threat would be when the channel was next dredged. It would only have seemed fruitless to Brian if the safe and, more importantly, whatever was inside it, had remained mere figments of his unreliable imagination. But it had existed and Brian now knew it was just a stone's throw from the western causeway and well within reach. Leaving the Victorian safe on the wreck where it had spent the previous 130 years, roughly ten nautical miles dead south of Newhaven, would have been what he would called fruitless. They could have returned with nothing. They also could have died.

As they were observing speed limit signs of five knots on the stillest waters they had enjoyed over the past four hours in a marine version of a paint mixer, Bill's curiosity rose.

"What did you say about that Receiver of Wreck thing before, Bri?"

"It's a person working for the taxman basically. I had to register the wreck with them when I first found it, pulling that fisherman's nets off the ribs of the hull."

"Right, I'm with you."

"So officially, we should register that find with them within 28 days and wait a year and a day for any surviving relatives of the owners to claim it."

"Why a year and a day, Bri?"

"It's an old maritime law."

"And if they don't come forward?" Bill asked expectantly, his inner pirate awakened.

"Then the taxman will get the salvage and me, the salvor gets close to bugger all. A "salvage award" they call it"

"Eh?"

"Yeah, it's bloody weird. And they wonder why things go missing? Oh and I may have needed a licence to bring the safe up too," Brian admitted, sheepishly.

"No wonder you left it there. Now I understand."

"But I'm just saving them time and money as there aren't any surviving relatives. I researched every document that the Receiver would, if I'd registered it."

"Blimey. What would have happened if those police had found us with it?" Bill was an otherwise responsible married father of two.

"We would've been a bit fucked there, Bill, if I'm honest with you. Big fines: maybe a sentence if the judge was in a bad mood!" By comparison, Brian was an unmarried, carefree, 46-year-old delinquent.

"Shit, why didn't you tell me that before, Bri?"

"I couldn't. Or, I mean, I didn't know the safe was gonna be there. Just had one of those hunches, you know? So when I found it, I couldn't leave it there."

"So you just left it where you did for safe keeping, ha ha."

The southerly wind, courier of the infinite showers, blew up the ever-narrowing mouth of the Ouse River. The only interruption to the shielded stretch of water was when the slab-sided Sealink car ferry departed for the daily crossing to Dieppe. It was 120 metres in length and 30 from their dinghy up to the peak of the pyramid-like funnel that poured out a heavy diesel smoke, many shades darker than the brightening sky. Brian's right arm was incessantly shifting the handle on the outboard motor to steer their dinghy over the forceful ridge of swell pushed out by the ferry's bow.

Feeling much like an ant below an elephant, Bill declared at a suitably raised volume, "That's a biggun', Bri!"

Behind them was the entrance of Newhaven, the concrete breakwater over their left shoulder. On the eastern side of the port stood a line of cranes loading or unloading piles of twisted scrap metal, before the timber wave attenuator, much like a pier without a boardwalk, began stretching into the Channel over their right shoulder. Shallow chalk cliffs surrounding the entire port were slowly emerging from the shadows. In front of them was the vacant berth from which they had "borrowed" their trusty dinghy, Brian hoped the owner wasn't standing there with more policemen, having reported it stolen. In the short distance that remained, Brian began to reflect on how much of a success their outing had proved, even if the safe wasn't up on dry land... yet.

He had been beset with a mental malaise after his decompression sickness in Brazil two years earlier; now he felt a clearing of some of the cognitive cobwebs. Rather than sitting indoors and worrying about what would befall him next, he had to get back out more and do, rather than thinking or worrying about doing. Just go and do! The drama had reignited his adventure lust, which hadn't completely been extinguished, although it had reduced to a smoulder. His success at passing his diving fitness test, in the face of all sane opinion, be it medical or rational, had been lost in the frenzy of bringing the safe closer ashore and avoiding attention in doing so.

Chattering on idle revs, Brian cut the engine as they reached their highly anticipated destination, among patch-worked lobster pots and tubs full of nets, which smelt of decay and diesel. As the two adventurers set foot back on land, Brian felt his partner needed a reward. They had met ten years before on board *Red Knickers*, the speedboat of Brian's brother-in-law, who claimed it was the fastest thing on the Thames Estuary at the time. The invitation had come from Bill's wife Pat, who was a friend of Brian's sister, Colleen. And through all their subsequent scrapes and adventures, whether stealing Brian's boat back from impoundment by Spanish customs or putting to sea five hours earlier that morning, nothing appeared to get Bill down. He was always chirpy, never grumpy and a competent navigator.

After tying off, Brian patted his accomplice on the back and said, "Fancy that fry-up I promised you? I reckon we've earned a drink too, don't you?"

03. Full English

Brian's car heater only managed to reach lukewarm on the short drive tracing the road along the harbour's edge. Snaking a path back out towards the western quay, Bill was beginning to shiver with the blast of cold air aimed at him. The Hope Inn was a double-storey art-deco pub painted magnolia, with a handsome curving balcony supported by swollen whitewashed pillars. The beckoning lights of a warm British hostelry shone through the Georgian windows. Behind the Hope Inn rose cliffs with patches of exposed weather-beaten chalk; on the opposite side of the road were dripping bench tables that wouldn't accommodate customers again until the following spring.

Through two central pillars, Brian paused at the front door, with his hand upright against the polished brass push-plate. Slightly above the intoxicated murmur and chinking glasses produced by early morning alcoholics, he said, "Don't mention the safe Bill, OK? Most of the punters in here could be out there in half an hour if they knew about it. Just call it "cake" or something, alright?"

Brian pushed the door open; the choking cloud of dusty dry heat, cooking oil, fried bacon and cigarette smoke that hit them was so potent it made their eyes weep. Through the haze, among the patrons huddled in groups more conspiratorial than conversational, they found an empty table and Brian offered his friend an adult beverage. In salutation of the impending Christmas season, tragic looking paper-chains and lengths of threadbare tinsel were suspended across the mock Tudor ceiling beams. Once surely white, the remaining ceiling and walls were now mustard yellow. Every small pane of the windows was plastered with thick condensation that glistened. A gaudy fruit machine chiming from the corner of the musicless bar blended with the sound of rustling morning newspapers – all being expertly filtered to page three, the one with the woman exposing her breasts. The headlines were about the militant miners' strike gripping the country.

"Get your jacket off and chuck it on that radiator. I'll order two fry-ups, what do you want to drink?"

"Cup of tea?"

"You can get stronger if you want?"

"Ah lovely. Breakfast of champions. A light and bitter please Bri. No, sod it, I think I need a rye whiskey please pal," Bill asked as he shed his clingy ski jacket like a sopping second skin.

"Magic."

"One light and bitter, rye whisky, a double cognac and two full English, please?" Crammed into the only space at the bar, facing a line of tempting beer pumps proffering Double Diamond, Hofmeister and Watney's wares, Brian watched the liquid section of his order land clumsily on the gridded plastic drip tray and was assured that the food would follow to their table. His fellow patrons at the bar sat with their grip tight around their chosen morning tipple, mostly wearing shiny-shouldered donkey jackets, presumably at the end of a shift in the harbour.

"Here you go, Bill. I got you both, looks like you need it."

"Nice place, Bri," Bill observed with great sarcasm. "Your local? I like the sticky carpet!" Having wedged the second of his shoes between his drying jacket on top of the radiator and the sill of the window they sat next to, Bill's displeasure became even more acute as his socks adhered to the floor.

"God no," Brian scratched at his bearded cheek and grinned, "I got to know it when I was working out of the port, salvaging the *Dalhousie* a couple of years back. It's only meant to be open for breakfast in the mornings, but I don't see much orange juice being served!"

In recognition of a partially successful mission in retrieving their potential treasure from the Channel and avoiding being drowned or getting arrested, Bill lifted his heavy dimpled pint glass by the handle and said, "Cheers, Bri. Good health."

As their glasses chinked together, two plates of food that would shorten their lives considerably arrived in front of them. Caramel-brown sausages, crispy rashers of bacon, baked beans, mushrooms, shiny fried eggs, black pudding, tomato and a slice of fried bread – the full English and much deserved.

"Corrrrr, look at that!" Bill cried, excitedly rubbing his palms together before lowering his tone. "So what are you going to do with the cake, Bri? Go back and pick it up?"

Brian's eyes shot left and right instinctively before he leaned towards his salvage partner, "It should be OK there for a while, it'll sink rather than get shifted anywhere now.

We could just collect the centre, slice by slice, rather than the whole cake."

Bill noted the use of the word "we" and hoped, for the sake of his children and his own liberty, that Brian was employing the royal "we", as in the first person. Bill suspected he had more grey hairs on his head than when they had set off, not to mention the strands that had surely fallen out and possibly a few more wrinkles. "And you don't know what's in it?"

"No I haven't seen it yet. I felt a few ridges inside before lashing the rope around it. Something valuable enough to be placed in there. Time will tell."

Bill lowered his voice further. "And you say we should declare that cake, officially?"

"Yeah and then end up with bugger all basically."

"Pretty stacked in their favour, eh Bri?"

"Just for stamping a form while we're risking our bollocks out there. If they wanted such a big share, maybe they should go and get it themselves." Bill found this impossible to disagree with.

"You'll be able to buy another Maserati, Bri?"

"No way. That *baastard* cost me a bloody fortune. Maybe another boat though."

A few joyous mouthfuls of oily fried meats later with the Cognac having lowered his reserve, Brian felt the need to come clean. The encouragement of surviving his dive had been overlooked, lost in the frenetic return to shore.

Perhaps he wasn't as unemployable as he and his doctor had feared he was.

"That was the first time I've been under the water in over two years."

"Eh? What do you mean, two years?"

"I got a decompression sickness in Brazil. A bend, you know? But a bad one. I could have ended up in a wheelchair."

"Fuck, two years! Has it been that long? What happened, Bri?" Bill asked, absorbing the shocking news. He could still see what he had first felt since meeting Brian earlier that morning – he seemed to have lost just a little of his usual zest, but he had been putting it down to his diving exertions combined with the ageing process. Brian's hunger for adventure, rugged confidence and ability to get away with it, appeared undimmed. He still had the capacity to bullshit with the best of 'em and his heart-throb smile intact. He still stuck his chin out when thinking, or nervous, or both, and his humour was drier than ever. The dimensions of his balls clearly hadn't reduced.

"It was me and my bell partner, Malcolm, a good South African guy I worked out there with. Our last dive was 290m, close to 1,000 feet and decompression went very fucking wrong. It took nearly 10 days to get us back up to the surface in the chamber. We had a few issues."

"Like what, Bri?"

"Normally, there are rest stops when they hold you at a certain pressure before continuing. There weren't any of those. Malcolm had a bad knee bend first, which held us up a little."

"Fuck!"

"Then near the surface, Malcolm become paralysed temporarily and I passed out. I had a cerebral decompression sickness diagnosed. And while this was all happening, the dive supervisor and ship doctor fucked off and were pissing it up in Copacabana. So I took the *baastards* on and they paid me $50,000, out of court."

"Bloody hell, Bri."

"We could've, and should've died in there. So I'm a lucky *baastard*. We both were."

"What's Malcolm doing now? Did he also recover?"

"Yeah he did. As far as I know, Malcolm's still working, but I haven't seen or heard from him since."

"Does your family know, Bri?"

"No, haven't mentioned it. Just easier for me that way."

"So what have you been up to for two years?"

"Just resting. I had to hang around in Rio for six months waiting for the case to come to court. Been having treatment or scans back here since and just laying low." Brian's version of sedentary stasis also involved his invitation to work on a video survey of the entire *Titanic* wreck, with a chance to buy into the project. "My brain basically remapped itself. I had lots of headaches. A lot of the *baastards,* sometimes for days." Brian's next sentence was a mark of his continued recovery and the fact he felt it was perhaps time to engage more with the world. "But I'm getting bored of just going to the gym and calling the weightlifters a bunch of "pussies" when I walk in."

"You don't, do you, Bri?" Bill chuckled. Brian nodded with a broad smile as he drained the glass tumbler for his second breakfast cognac, revelling in his own stupidity.

By the time Bill was dragging pieces of fried bread across his empty plate like a squeegee, he had heard the whole sorry story. The listless symptoms, the chronic fatigue, the hyperbaric therapy, neurological assessments, the cerebral fog, blurred vision and memory lapses - to the degree Brian would often forget where he lived and had once forgotten how to drive, while at the wheel of his Maserati. His doctor had strongly advised him against any further diving, but Bill suggested another approach that Brian's physician might concur with.

"Well, with your experience, couldn't you supervise from now on, managing the divers?"

"No, I wouldn't be comfortable doing that. I could have another black out while responsible for four guys in a chamber next door."

"Well, yeah. That does make sense, since you put it like that, Bri. How about giving up just the deep saturation diving then?"

"Back to how I started? Maybe you have a point, Bill."

"You were diving a few hours ago and you seem OK to me, pal. You survived didn't you?" Bill offered, as an attempted pep talk.

Brian had not only survived; he thrived living a life beyond the comprehension of most. Normality was a boring prospect. He had spent such a large portion of his life risking it, and invoicing accordingly, that uncertainty had become a comfort against otherwise mundane demands of life. Bill had made a very valid suggestion. Brian needed to get moving, get his claws stuck into the world again. He could seek shallow coastal or civil engineering diving. The type of work that opened the gateway to commercial diving that he charmed and lied his way into in London's docks in 1970, 14 years earlier. And just as in his early jobs, the only person he would be placing at risk was himself.

Rather than just watching the constant flow of money out of his accounts, Brian could resume bringing some in. The experienced diving fraternity were knit tightly along the southern coast, so a couple of phone calls was all that would be required. The cinders of his former self just needed fanning with a dose of sea stimulation and the adrenaline rush of avoiding a custodial sentence. Some adventurous salvage therapy had already put the wind back in his sails; a superior treatment to anything his doctor may prescribe. Brian's path back to a more normal working life had been seeded by his friend's advice. It was time to move forward and indulge in less contemplation, looking in the rear view mirror.

The corners of Brian's mouth began to lift to a smile. "Thanks, Bill. A problem shared is a problem doubled, they say!"

"Shouldn't you buy a place now, with that pay-out from Brazil and whatever the contents of the cake is? You can't keep renting if you'll be around more now."

Brian couldn't disagree with the counsel, but the boost to his finances also meant he could risk it all again with a buy-in on the *Titanic* project. His earlier self would glaze over when normal things like buying houses were proposed. However, he was 46 and had to stop behaving like an overgrown delinquent at some point. Tenancy agreements were a mechanism for him to accrue months' worth of rent arrears. To this end, he had lost another two apartments and the contents thereof in France and Brazil. His large saturation diving pay cheques had been spent on fast cars, boats and the company of women; the rest he had wasted on salvage projects that might have offered him a career, post diving.

"Can I perhaps offer you some dry roasted peanuts for dessert, sir?"

"No, Bri. I need to get going back soon."

Brian had options to contemplate and phone calls to get on with. Bill was dry and keen to return to a domestic life, for another couple of years at least. Or until Brian was next in touch. A morning of Brian's life was more than enough for Bill for the next year. He would labour to remember a time when he had been more petrified than when bobbing around a busy shipping lane in an unlit dinghy, unaware if his friend was alive or dead some 40m below. His regular fix of fear was already being provided by his love of windsurfing out in the Thames estuary. He used a body harness that, when incorrectly attached, would launch him over the top of his sail with alarming frequency, like a medieval catapult. The craziest thing in Bill's usual life was the paving on his patio, and he wanted it to remain like that in the future.

04. River of Strife

Half-cut on a Monday morning, with Brian's confidence boosted by his sympathetic comrade, they parted back at Bill's car, which was parked outside Brian's penthouse in a corner of Brunswick Square in Brighton, formed by four-storey regency town houses sandwiched together in a U-shape. An angry wind carried salt mist up from the beach and noisily swirled through the bare branches of trees in the centre of the garden lawns as brave birds clung to them. Clouds in the sky were travelling at similar rates as the vehicles traversing the promenade, as if the earth was spinning faster than normal. Flushed from full stomachs and stimulated livers, the whites of their eyes were wet and rose coloured. Brian leant into the open door of Bill's car, with his elbows outstretched on the wet roof and the top of the doorframe, shielding him from the intemperate morning as the shipmates bid each other a farewell.

"Yeah, I gotta get home to have a kip, Bri. I'm whacked and the kids will be home from school about three."

"Say hello to Pat from me."

"Yeah I will. And that's all I will be telling her about this morning. I need a shower to wash all the shit out of my strides, pal."

"It did get a bit..." A snigger punctured the delivery of the last word of Brian's sentence, "...hairy!"

"And don't forget Bri, get on the phone and see what work you can get locally, just to get yourself out and about again. Forget the crazy deep stuff from now on, maybe? Have a ring around and turn down nothing, pal. And give me a shout when you're ready to finish what we started this morning?" Bill said with a wink, much to Brian's surprise.

"Magic, mate, I will."

Brian closed Bill's car door and followed with a couple of friendly taps on the glass before crossing the road to his apartment. From the top of six rounded steps at the entrance to his regency apartment block, Brian watched Bill start his homeward journey around the square, following a whining milk float. He left a trail of exhaust steam and gave a hoot of his horn. Brian waved to send him off. Providing just as much motivation as Bill's encouraging words was the eviction notice that greeted him as Brian finished climbing the spiral staircase around the lift shaft.

"*Baastard!*"

While Brian was occupied out in the Channel, the locks had been clinically changed during the swift repossession; the notice was stuck below the spy hole on his front door with a drawing pin. As the flat would be reported as unoccupied at the time of repossession, it confirmed the landlord's suspicion that the reason for non-payment of rent was that the tenant had died or absconded, or was serving a prison sentence. Therefore, Brian's first phone call would be a faux grovelling one to his surprised landlord, made from the nearest phone box on the promenade. More northern cursing continued as he descended the staircase and read more of the notification.

"*Baastard*... Bollocks... *Baastard!*"

Within three days, having regained entry to his penthouse, upon the promise of settling the unpaid rent, Brian was turning down a slew of job offers. These included diamond diving in Namibia, which, despite the glamourous name, was essentially akin to vacuuming up the seabed onto a processing ship, in shark-infested waters at the mouth of the Orange River. The other offer that had had to be refused was a job inland, which would have been his preference, if it hadn't been unclogging waste gates in sewage treatment tanks. He did accept a "river job" even though no other details were given, as it was relatively close by in Surrey.

Beyond a taped-off police cordon, in a small gravelled car park adjacent to Chertsey Bridge, Brian went to report himself for duty. A bustling thoroughfare supported by five limestone arches rose up and over a narrow stretch of the Thames River in Surrey, to the south west of London. Unsure of police protocols, Brian stood within earshot of a pre-recovery briefing, close enough to suggest he was due to be involved, as he learnt the grim specifics of the task he had hastily accepted.

Footpaths, edge fencing, rubbish bins and even an unlucky young lad in a boat had all been swallowed by the raised water levels. The river was nearly twice its normal width, and the tops of slatted back benches and footpath signs that broke the foamy surface were the only clue to the normal course of the river. Two pubs on either muddy bank were still to open that morning, as the traffic ebbed over the crossing. A crowd of curious dog walkers mixed with schoolchildren was growing on the cap of the bridge, drawn by the flashing blue lights of police cars and rescue vehicles assembling below them. A group of concerned relatives were huddled in a corner of the car park near the raging river, letting out the occasional wail of heartache. A police liaison officer was walking back and forth to the gathered friends and family members, providing updates and what comfort he could in the tragic circumstances.

The officer leading the briefing paused momentarily and leant backwards for a clearer view of the stranger with the leather jacket and freshly trimmed horseshoe moustache. "Are you Brian?"

"Yep," Brian uneasily concurred. His natural instinct to provide a false name always made him pause before confirming his actual name.

"Great. We need to get you suited up and in the water. But please join us, we're just running through how we'll recover the body."

No one in the group envied Brian's task as they all ambled down to the river's edge, where vortexes spun gurgling pockets of small branches, polystyrene, plastic bottles and punctured footballs. The whirlpool adjacent to where Brian was due to commence his day's work contained a dead rotating swan. The par-boiled surface of the Thames moved forcefully downstream, away from the crossing, belying the strength of currents which Brian would encounter beneath the surface. The water level had already begun to drop; it no longer breached the lock, upstream on the opposite side of the bridge. Cylindrical birch trees followed the bend in the river downstream across normally open meadows. The drooping arms of willow trees were dragged taut into the water, like lines from fishermen's rods.

The torrential rain of the previous days, the cause of the flooding, abated as the search and recovery operation began. Considering the state of the river, scuba tanks would be used; an umbilical would add too much drag to the diver and could snag on large objects. A rope had already been tethered over the river for Brian to attach himself to as he worked across the waterway as best he could. Clad in his trusty burgundy dry suit, Brian stood knee-deep in the river. The current below the surface was powerful. His air tank was mounted upside down, with the valve easier to reach, a method he preferred from his experience diving offshore.

"Poor lad. Who would think to take a canoe out in weather like this, eh? Only 10 years old," The commanding officer observed in a removed "rather you than me" tone. Brian didn't greatly appreciate the summary of his task; he had a nephew of the same age. "Right, we have a vehicle either side of the river with a rope tied between them as you can see. Attach yourself to that pulley with your rope and adjust it as you work across on a tight line. That way we can move them six feet further down river and you can work your way back across and sweep the whole section." This sounded straightforward enough.

To finish dressing himself, Brian was assisted as he lifted his mustard yellow helmet up and over his head to fasten it to the chromed circular housing of his rubberised neck scarf. Once fitted, without the usual communications to a diving bell or supervisor up on the support vessel, he was alone with his thoughts and rightly voiced a question to himself; "Brian, what the fuck are you doing, you dozy *baastard*?"

As he took a first step, the current nearly forced him over, so he dropped forward into the river to begin his first grisly crossing, sightlessly exploring the riverbed with his hands. Turbulent, unreadable currents and tows twisted him left and right, up and down, and grew stronger the deeper he went. Using his torch was pointless in the muddied, angry water judging by the view through the glass faceplate in his helmet. His body was continually struck with objects, those aimed at his helmet thumped loudly against its fibreglass shell. Brian knew another pass across the river was complete as he threaded himself through the weed growing at the regular water's edge and began to feel what would normally be the steep grassy banks. On his third crossing, having only groped at a shopping trolley, a rusted motorbike frame and a tree stump on the riverbed, he was winded when a timber beam struck his lower ribs and left pelvis like a battering ram.

"Ahhh, you *baastard*," he winced, drawing extra air against the pain. The cold water provided few numbing qualities as he waited for the throbbing agony to subside before nervously palpating his trunk to check for any broken bones.

Brian found the body on his fifth pass. It was snagged against the sawn branches of a coppiced tree stump the size of a whisky barrel. He got a fright when he felt the lifeless forearm first and recoiled momentarily, like an arachnophobe handling a spider. Feeling fatigued, cold and underpaid on a day rate a fraction of his offshore salad days, Brian moved his jaw forward and drew down his brow in contemplation. The scare increased his breathing rate, louder than any time that morning as his lungs pushed and pulled through the regulator valve. Facing into the current, at the full mercy of what the darkened Thames was sending his way, he grabbed the arm and started to pull upwards while bracing both his feet on the rounded remnant of an oak tree.

For fear of having to begin the search all over again, once it was freed Brian maintained a vice-like grip on that lifeless limb as he made for the churning surface. If he had let go in those conditions, the most prudent location to resume the search would have been the other side of London. Like an umbrella in a gale, the small body acted like a sail in the water as Brian aimed for the nearest bank. Rescue personnel and police officers rushed in Brian's direction, having noticed he had surfaced mid-river.

With vision returned on the river's edge, Brian averted his gaze as he sat chest deep while the body was handed over and removed from the river behind him. Unconfined shrieks of sorrow rang out as the parents of the deceased dashed over to grab their child, who was soon enveloped by the group that re-formed around the parents as their mourning began.

Five minutes later Brian was finally back out of the water and sitting next to his helmet, on the rear hatch of a police Range Rover painted white with a broad orange belt along each flank. Following a near two-year medical hiatus from diving, he was exhausted, having survived three hours of the rigours of a river determined to either drown or pelt him with its contents.

Supping thoughtfully from a much-deserved cup of hot, sugary tea and smoking a cigarette, he was daydreaming, watching a group of confused ducks waddle around the busy car park. He noted the sounds of raw grief had curtailed markedly as one of the tearful relatives left the group and sheepishly approached the commanding officer. The officer then walked in Brian's direction across the cordoned-off car park; he presumed it was to pass on the families' gratitude. But Brian was wrong.

"Err, Brian. Sorry to interrupt your well-earned break, but it appears you may have recovered the wrong body," the officer said. He sounded as confused and bewildered as Brian was. His first reaction was to tip his head over his left shoulder in realisation the task was not complete after all. Before Brian could respond, the officer broke the obvious news. "So you'll have to go back in; sorry!"

05. Far Flung Finances

Brian inspected his badly bruised hip, the lateral haematoma a swirl of browns and purples, with raised scarlet inflammation marking the point where the timber beam had smashed into his flank as it travelled downriver. A crispy packet of frozen peas was bringing some relief as he sat inelegantly smoking a cigarette. His occasional lunges for the ashtray carried painful involuntary grunts. Shallow breathing counteracted the discomfort from his bruised ribs; laughing or coughing had quite the opposite effect and was most unwelcome.

The bottle of cognac Brian had drained the remaining three shots from to recuperate after the double body recovery the previous day still sat on the coffee table. Beside a balloon glass clouded with fingerprints was a spent blister pack of paracetamol that contained two remaining pills. Brian washed them down with a gulp of warm tea. A wall clock ticked along noisily on the wall above the draylon sofa. It hadn't been his first taste of recovering remains from a watery grave, but if he never had to do it again, Brian wouldn't be too upset. However, that was dive number two of his recovery, admittedly in a veritable puddle compared to the depths he had last been working in Brazil, but it was all encouraging. His physical contusions and muscle spasms would ease in a few more days. And the reordered contents of his head, the site of medical examination, scans and conjecture since that last deep dive, were yet to object to Brian's gradual re-introduction to work. He knew he had to get back on the horse; otherwise, he never would again.

A far larger body blow was delivered by his Harley Street doctor, Dr John King, later the same morning. He had phoned to update Dr King on his recent work activities and the fact that he had had no ill effects or headaches. But by the end of the call, Brian had greater concerns, which for most patients would have been worthy of a course of Diazepam and an extended period of lying down in a darkened room.

"That's excellent news Brian. I'm pleased you're feeling ready to take on the world again. Great news. But please, just stay away from the deep stuff. I don't think your brain would respond well to that again. I'm glad you phoned actually, as I meant to contact you this week. It appears our charming accountant on Jersey may have done a runner with our money! Did you know?"

"What? I'm due to get over there soon, Doc," Brian asked, grinding his canine teeth together, fearful of the doctor's non-medical triage.

"Going to visit your monies over there, Brian, were you?" Dr King said, in a jocular manner that seemed inappropriate given the gravity of his news. Brian's monies totalled £65,000 and Dr King's own retirement plans would have to be postponed.

"I've been trying to get the *baastard* on the phone for the past few days."

"Yes, me too."

"Now I know why I couldn't. Shit!"

"Not the greatest news just before Christmas, eh? I found out two days ago. We aren't alone, I'm afraid, there are twelve of us that I know about, but it could be more. He won't be answering the phone Brian. Apparently he's in the Far East somewhere already. Nearly 800 grand they reckon."

"Does the dumb *baastard* have any idea who he's ripped off? Jesus, I wouldn't have the balls to try that."

"Indeed. I've met many of your brethren in passing from performing medicals and examinations: a formidable bunch certainly. But you'll know them better than me from your diving days. I couldn't think of a better debt collection agency, could you?"

Having spent up to six weeks at a time in a compression chamber with many of his fellow victims, Brian was more aware than most of the risks their financial advisor had exposed himself to. "Well, I don't fancy his chances."

"I wouldn't bet that he'll make it to next Christmas, Brian. Do you?"

"I wouldn't bet he'll make even next year, Doc."

Brian had been using the Jersey-based auditor to arrange his fiscal affairs since a friend had recommended him on his first trip out into the North Sea. Brian had felt the need due to the sudden increase in danger-pay. He was bookkeeper to many of Brian's colleagues from that pioneering era, who were dotted all over the world. On the back of Brian's overly trusting nature, the appearance of his accountant and that of his company in Jersey was of someone in a position of trust. He had seemed like a pillar of the community, much like Dr King. That was until the accountant's discreet taste for gambling on horse racing, the only outlet for a legal flutter on the island, grew beyond what his own finances could bear. Signing a "lasting power of attorney" agreement with the firm in 1975 to facilitate tax payments or rebates on the mainland nine years earlier, had proven to be a fateful decision… and a foolish one. However convenient it may have appeared to a globetrotting saturation diver.

The accountant had unwittingly chosen the wrong set of clients to pilfer from, compared to his normal client base of retired channel islanders. Many of them had significant hand-to-hand combat experience, and that's not to mention their furious wives. Brian was a former nightclub manager, attempted armed robber, illustrator and latter day commercial diver, but almost all of his colleagues were ex-special forces, navy seals and marines, who would be extremely imaginative and resourceful in such economic circumstances. Although no pushover himself in comparison, Brian could merely charm people to death. It wasn't if, but merely when the accountant would be found. It was only a matter of time. The case would certainly not be pursued through the courts. There would be no claim and counter argument heard, zero cross-examination, and negotiation would be waived. The accountant was a dead man walking, somewhere in the tropics.

Until then Brian's entire life savings in Jersey were missing, for the time being at least. However, his feast and famine approach to living arrangements and finances had been ample training for the uncertainty ahead. After 14 years of commercial diving, the reflex to panic in a tight spot had been long overcome, for it was the most effective way to kill yourself underwater. So he wouldn't be fretting if his nest egg from that career were momentarily frozen, however perturbing it appeared when Dr King delivered the news. His sole source of accessible liquidity was now narrowed down to the illegally recovered safe, stuck at the bottom of a muddy channel at the western approach to Newhaven harbour. Then the encrusted contents of it would still have to be melted down.

The consequences of this grenade exploding in his finances, however short a period of time it might be before appropriate recourse was exacted upon the accountant's person, began to align itself once the initial shock of the news from his doctor waned. Now the only way he could be involved in the project to complete a video survey of the entire wreck of the *Titanic* would be as an employee, rather than a bought-in stakeholder. There was never any spilt milk to cry over in Brian's mind; problems only existed to be assessed and surmounted with style. The ache on his left side had become a secondary concern, as Brian now had greater problems. No matter how often he was jarred by the injury when thoughtlessly reaching for a notepad or retrieving a business card holder from his leather briefcase.

Within an hour, the cream handset of his trimphone was wedged between his cheek and shoulder as Brian's bent index finger dialled the number of his dependable and fellow rogue salvage artist.

Bill answered the phone in characteristic style: "Hello, you've reached the Samaritans". It was a support service Brian could probably have benefitted from.

"Hello, it's Bri. How are you doing?" Brian replied through a therapeutic grin.

"Oh, still above ground, pal. How you doing, Bri?" Bill couldn't remember a time when Brian had just called for a chat.

"Magic, my old mate."

"You're not phoning me from prison are ya, pal?"

"Ahh, don't make me laugh. I hurt my side yesterday working in the Thames in Surrey. Ah."

"Oh, you been working already, pal?"

"Yeah, but we have to finish off that job in Newhaven sooner than planned, if you're still keen?"

Bill spun his body into the corner of the room, pretending to look for something as he murmured out the corner of his clasped mouth, "Is it illegal again this time, Bri?"

"I'm not going to lie. Probably yes!"

"Ok, when do you need a hand, pal? Please say soon as Pat has got me gluing tinsel around the bloody light switches here."

"If you can do it this side of Christmas, that'd be magic."

"I'll speak to Pat and let you know, pal. I know she has us going to a dinner and dance one night before Christmas."

"And there's one more thing."

"What's that, Bri?"

"Can I borrow a couple of grand to tide me over? My accountant has done a runner with my readies. I…"

Bill interrupted, "Jesus Christ Bri. The one in Jersey? Are you serious?"

"It's not as bad as it sounds, luckily, he's done it to a lot of the divers I used to work with and most of them aren't very nice people if you piss them off. So the *baastard* will be found soon and dealt with."

"No problem, pal. I'll bring the cash with me when I come down to you, OK."

"Magic, Bill. You're a star. I couldn't afford the hook to hang my arse on otherwise!"

Brian couldn't face the eye-rolling disapproval involved with applying for another loan from the Worley family bank. His alien lifestyle and ability to earn were incomprehensible to those in the ordinary nine-to-five world. Now Bill was providing overdraft facilities, on top of an apparent willingness to defraud the British exchequer in Brian's latest scheme. Listening to the continuing run of bad luck Brian was a party to, it seemed an act of mercy for Bill to assist his friend once again. Brian's livelihood, flashy Maserati Merak and *Highroller*, the motor cruiser he had relocated to the port of Cassis in France, had all disappeared since Bill had last seen his audacious friend. All the consequence of a single decompression in Brazil, a process Brian had undergone safely many times before. Until Brazil, life had been a system that Brian had gamed fairly well; a series of events through which he would hopefully prosper. He had been playing a high-stakes game of chance, which had been particularly pulsating when he was exiting a diving bell 300 metres beneath the surface. He had been playing poker with his own life. Failure wasn't a tattoo; it was a bruise that would heal, just like the inflammation on the upper crest of his pelvis. As long as Brian had pleasant company on his arm, access to enough funds to keep him in decent cognac and good Italian shoes, there were no pressing financial concerns on his mind.

It was a week before Christmas and he was yet to buy a single present for his nieces and nephews. However, that was nothing a frenetic, guerrilla-like visit to the high street nearest his mother's house wouldn't address. Something fluffy or flashing with "sonic" written on it for those who still believed in Santa Claus. Cash folded inside a Christmas card for older gawky teenage non-believers. A wink and a tap to the side of his nose would accompany the opening of each gift from their crazy uncle.

But before the familial festivities in Essex commenced, Brian had to refill his scuba tanks, borrow an amphibious metal detector, find a compass, some metal bars and buy a new lift bag to finally bring the *Dalhousie* loot back onto land, 130 years later and 14,000 miles short of its intended destination: Sydney, Australia.

06. Dangerous Drift

"And you found the wrong body? Christ, how many were in there, Bri?"

Brian didn't speculate on this, he had pulled out two and that had been unpleasant enough. He was informing Bill of his return to diving work in the Thames as they stopped every few paces near the end of the western quay of Newhaven harbour, reliving their fraught return to shore eight days earlier.

"That sounds terrible, Bri."

"You said turn nothing down, so I blame you," Brian said dryly, with just a hint of a tell-tale caddish smile.

Fishing lines, trampled, discarded bait and gull guano mixed with the spray that rose off the waves into weed-lined pools along the rutted top of the concrete finger curving out to sea. To their left, the portside waters were canal calm and reflective. To their right, an unwelcoming high tide bounced against the weather-side of the breakwater. A shifting Channel breeze blew from no particular and every direction. Apart from a dishevelled and, more importantly, uninterested fisherman nearer to shore, they were alone. The winter sun was draped low in the sky and made fleeting appearances through breaks in the clouds, illuminating the mist blanketing the port.

Brian had applied himself and managed to source a fishing trolley, primarily designed to shoulder sea-angling equipment from the car. His carried a brace of scuba tanks, his dry suit, a lightened helmet, weight belt, a thick length of reinforcing bar and a metal detector that he hoped wouldn't be needed, all wrapped in a canvas lift bag. Brian hadn't noted any significant storms visiting the coast since their triumphant drink in the Hope Inn, so he remained confident the safe would still be in situ. He had less certainty about taking the direct route to the booty, watching wave after wave punch against the wild side of the harbour wall. The eruptions of spray scattered indignant clusters of sea birds as they sought a safe standpoint near the edges, which was impossible in the conditions.

"Right, I reckon it's better to drop in the flat side and I'll scramble around the end and drop down into the channel where we left it and drift dive back here," Brian briefed as they quietly prepared on the end of the breakwater with line of sight to the marker buoy that had provided a secondary reference.

"Righto." Bill was only pretending that he understood what Brian was talking about. He listened with care, pleased they hadn't put to sea in another unsuitable craft that didn't actually belong to Brian. He shook his head from time to time in incredulity. "Are you sure you've recovered, Bri?" It was a sound question to pose, having fully evaluated Brian's salvage plans on location, which he hadn't shared during their phone call.

As he stepped into the sealed feet of his dry-suit, Brian replied, "I don't have much choice really." Which they both knew was true if Bill was going to get his loan repaid. "It's gonna be a *baastard* getting out there, as I'm going into the current. But easier getting back. Can you zip me up at the back here, Bill?" As the rubberised zip, dropping diagonally across Brian's shoulder, was closed, he signalled he was ready, "Magic. So it was 150, 200 feet off of here and roughly the same from that buoy?"

"That's right, Bri."

On went his twin tanks, braced together on a frame. He locked the lines into the valve on the right side of his helmet before it dropped down over his head. He left his flippers and lift bag behind. Bill would throw them out to him, still shaking his head, once Brian had traced the barnacled rusty rungs forming a ladder, cured into the concrete wall when first poured.

The water column that met Brian when he had rounded the irregular point of the breakwater was immense. Twin air pipes feeding his helmet immediately hummed as they oscillated together. Scrabbling across foundation rubble to dive under the western approach into Newhaven, he thought it prudent to drop as low as possible before setting off in the estimated direction of his target, minimising the effects of the swell and the running current. The extra effort would also reduce his time underwater. Brian kept his breathing steady and deep; his instinctive composure underwater overrode any itch to panic. The view through his helmet was an ever-shifting fawn miasma of suspended mud and seaweed clumps, sheared from their roots. A sunken car chassis, pontoon frame and an enormous anchor in Brian's turbulent path offered welcome purchase as he lugged his way down deeper towards the dredged bed. His gloves were obscured when reaching out for his next hold traversing the sunken castoffs. His grip kept tightening and loosening in relation to his orientation to the current that gave him a constant bearing. Working to maintain the flow of water against his uninjured right side was his most effective way to position himself in the correct area.

Like a sightless man in a hurricane, Brian felt and fumbled with every limb for the cubed corners of the safe before driving both hands into the mud to move himself forward, sideways, or backwards, whatever direction the current nudged him in. When it momentarily ceased, he was showered with a cascade of shingle. The flat, featureless bottom of the dredged passage offered no shield to Brian as he explored the area, with the fortitude of a man recently defrauded out of £65,000.

The radiating drone from the propeller of a large vessel was unmistakable and growing worryingly in volume above his head. Brian grabbed at the first solid object he found; the large metal ring of a cement-filled oil drum. He held on and closed his eyes, steadying his breathing and waiting for the quaking judder and growl of the engines to reach their peak. Holding on for dear life amid the deafening swoosh of the turning brass blades, his helmet was repeatedly slammed into the object chocking the cylindrical drum. To soften the impending impact, as his neck was beginning to jar, he extended out his right palm as a brace.

Following its hasty return to the deep when Brian had cut the rope, the safe had landed on its side with one edge beginning to slump into the yielding mud, so it looked more like a triangular chest, with an oil drum and some snagged tangerine fishing net for company. When the current allowed, Brian could probe the corroded safe to confirm he could jettison the metal detector, which had been hindering his journey. He grasped through the sole accessible side and felt down the exterior for the feet, confirming the find.

"Bullseye, you *baastard*!"

Once his right fist stopped shaking in understandable triumph, he reached inside to find the entire space packed with silt.

"Bollocks."

Brian was back in business, until he checked his air gauge. One tank had been nearly spent reaching the site but the recovery and return remained. His lift-bag, wrapped around the re-bar tucked in his weight belt to reduce his resistance, was the next to go. There was little point using precious air to inflate a leaky lift bag if it would be much better used keeping him alive. With his left hand still welded to the ring on the oil drum, he scooped out what he could from the safe with his right. Several handfuls later, his breathing was becoming harder, so switched the supply to his helmet to the second tank before reaching for the rebar he'd let fall under his knees. The inside of the strongbox and whatever contents had fused to it now felt clear enough to introduce some brute persuasion. Brian fed the far end of the bar into the rusted aperture and began pounding at the contents from every possible angle, driving the rod back inside, the movement of every blow finished with a damaging blunt thud against the caked contents. A final pommel jammed the bar between the lead-soft cargo. Unable to extract the rod, he began levering it in circular motions against whatever remained in the safe. The bar bent under the pressure until it released.

His curiosity was piqued. With his finite stocks of air reducing with each breath he took, Brian dropped the rod and returned his hand back inside. He felt one, then two, a third and then the final fourth ingot. They all felt smooth and free of crud, maybe too uncontaminated for silver given they had spent 130 years enclosed in an oxidising box forged from a dissimilar metal. They were about wrist thick and as long as his hand, each thinned to the width of a thumb through their scooped centre. And they were hopelessly heavy without a lift bag.

Brian lifted one up to his helmet for a closer inspection among the bubbles. It did look like silver and was relatively uniform, given how much force had been needed to loosen them. Brian dropped his initial find between his legs and grabbed another one, then another until four silvery ingots were hastily piled together. Whatever the haul was, it was time to bring it back to dry land. Now he just had to work out how to reach Bill with the extra weight. The thought did cross his mind that if his air ran out, he was as good as dead. A mystery corpse of a diver, overloaded with plundered precious metal.

In an effort to avoid that outcome, Brian began to dig under the shingle where the drum and the safe met until there was a void large enough to jam his left foot and shin. Once tight and secured, he closed his right knee against the other side of the safe, like loppers around a thick branch. His hands met either side of the clasp of his weight belt and slid it open before pulling it around to rest on his groin. He then threaded each of the individual weights off the canvas webbing before returning the empty band around his injured waist. Then he swiftly placed the bars between the loose belt and his dry suit. Brian had to tension the buckle to keep the bars snug against his trunk, further gripped by the weave of the fabric providing a key for the pitted surface of the bars.

In excess of what they had replaced, both in terms of weight and price per ounce on the open market, Brian gave the belt a final tug to test it would last the 200 feet return trip to where Bill was patiently waiting. It would help if he kept his lungs as full as possible for the duration; the more air there was inside him, the more buoyant his overladen body would be. His underestimation of his air consumption was a hidden blessing as escorting a lift-bag to shore in those conditions would be as unsettling as opening a parachute on a windy hilltop.

Bill didn't see Brian scrabble, swim, bodysurf, tumble and drag himself out of the channel. He couldn't inform Brian of the incoming Dieppe ferry, which looked as if it sailed right over where Brian had set out for. Nor could he alert him to the same police cruiser that had challenged them on their return to Newhaven, circling the distant area. Nonetheless, it was a far a less traumatic shift as Brian's vicarious dive support, he thought. Bill had run through all his methods for not attracting suspicion as somebody loitering on their own at the end of the harbour's breakwater. His thick sheepskin coat and flat-cap didn't give him the look of a patient angler. But he had paced back and forth, then rested his hands on the railing as if he was looking for the best spot to cast into. He had checked his watch many times out of concern, before settling on just sitting in the empty trolley.

Bill first saw Brian emerge from around the point of the breakwater after nearly an hour and a half. He looked like a creature from the deep but was unnoticed by others in the shifting mist. Brian climbed the rungs out of the water with all four ingots safely in place, thus completing an undeclared withdrawal from the Bank of Salvage, free from VAT and whatever other charges the Receiver of Wreck might care to levy. Water drained from every part of his profile as Brian detached his air hoses and began loosening his helmet. Apart from his right shoulder and arm, Brian's entire being was layered in a black, stagnant substance he hoped was mud.

"That's a very wet looking man in that dry suit, Bri. Christ, I thought you had popped it. The ferry came in 20 minutes after you left and I had no way of telling you, pal."

"It's OK, I knew it was there. I'm fucking freezing," Brian replied loudly. "Don't worry, I made it," he finished, sarcastically stating the obvious.

"I was starting to think about who to call about a missing diver. Did you find it?"

In answer to Bill's interest Brian swiftly drew the bars pinned to his trunk by his belt, each landing with a substantial clunk in the base of the trolley as his grin grew. He pressed the final ingot into Bill's hands with a wink. There was such a discrepancy between the weight Bill expected and what actually loaded into his hands, he nearly dropped it to the floor.

"Christ, Bri. What's that?

Brian's arms were raised over his head, preparing to lift off his helmet. "I'm not 100% yet. But let's get it to the car. I need a large bloody cognac. Just keep *schtum* about this, OK?" was his obstructed appraisal.

07. Partner Poser

Weighing a seemingly impossible two kilos given their form, the four matte bars dried out on the circular table in the bay window of his penthouse, while Brian sought a maritime mover for his find. He rung around associates dotted along the south coast, people he had come across during the ill-fated salvage of the *Dalhousie* wreck. He wanted them to refer him to someone who could shift the merchandise onto a willing dealer with no questions asked, for a fee. For three days, he returned to the table to inspect one ingot or another. An oxidized hallmark was visible on each, although they were nearly indiscernible. They would have been much clearer when the safe was originally loaded and locked in London in 1853. If the *Dalhousie* had completed the voyage to Australia, where would the bars have found themselves? Roughly cast, with notable irregularities from each other; he studied the distinctions in weight and finish and surface contours, during his constant viewings.

A low-key pub lunch, then a discreet dinner meeting led to a cloak-and-dagger midnight introduction to a mysterious Swiss man at the head of Brighton Palace Pier. During an inconspicuous rendezvous that would have been more appropriately staged against a crossing of the Berlin Wall, a cloth bank bag wrapped around the cumbersome bars was handed to a tall bespectacled man in a dark trench coat. Brian had been assured his launderer was called Christian, almost certainly falsely (in both name and nature). But he was definitely the kind of shadowy man able to convert hard-fought salvaged material into financial gain.

"I *vill* be in touch *zoon* on *ze* purity *und* value, *ja*? *Ve* meet back here *vhen* I have *ze* cash, *ja*?" These were the only words he said, in an austere Germanic accent, making it sound a routine business arrangement. No future times or dates were furnished. After a firm handshake and a shared nod beside a fish & chips kiosk, the bars were gone. With them off his hands and in the clear for now, Brian walked back along the short pier a little lighter in step, with the load of tax evasion and damning proof thereof lifted from his shoulders. Always willing to roll his dice, he had just handed over his latest, potentially greatest fortune to a shady Swiss fence whose ringed fingers were in many black market pies. The endorsements of his services by two of Brian's comrades who had also used Christian, gave him ample assurance of the man's abilities to swiftly exchange the goods for an untraceable currency of his choice. Brian had limited options and paying the bars into his bank account at the local branch wasn't one of them.

Next morning, he was jolted awake by the shrill, cheeping ring of his trimphone.

"Is that you Brian?" asked the South African voice of his former bell partner, Malcolm, the last person Brian had been in saturation with in Brazil. It was an echo of the world from which Brian had withdrawn since his cerebral decompression sickness.

"Yeah, who's that?" Brian asked while replaying Malcolm's voice in his head; initially, he was unable to place it.

"It's Mally. How you doing, my old china? I got your number from a mate I was on a course with in Aberdeen last week. Sorry if I woke you…"

"Sorry Malcolm. I was up a bit late last night, meeting a man about a horse, you know. How are you doing?"

"I'm OK, Brian. I bumped into a Brazilian colleague of ours in a pub in Aberdeen. Rodrigo, remember?

"No, sorry. Can't remember the name."

"Anyway, he told me your story with the lawyers and shit. I hadn't heard from you since, partner. Your lawyer got in touch though."

"Yeah, thanks for sending the decom sheet you ripped off their printer on the ship. That really helped."

"You're welcome. I never heard anything after that though."

"I had to take the *baastards* on after what they did to us."

"I don't blame you. I had to go back to work. I've got a wife and kids. I should've done the same as you though. You did the right thing."

"I got $50,000 off them in the end. Out of court, you know. They dragged it out for six months in Rio and paid out the morning of the case, right outside the assigned court. I even had to put a bloody suit on."

"Nice day rate that," Malcolm ribbed. He was allowed to joke about the fallout of their last decompression together, having been sat or slumped opposite Brian throughout their hellish ride back to the virtual surface, depending on how impaired they both were.

"Fucked me up afterwards, though."

"Doc King did my medical last week. He told me about the accountant doing a bunk too."

"Oh, fuck. Don't mention that, Mally. So actually, he's got my pay-out at the moment."

"Apparently, the guy has been tracked down to the Philippines somewhere. He won't last long," Malcolm switched the subject, aware his former colleague would be stinging from his recent loss. "But going back to Brazil, I was OK after a couple of days. My knees were stiff for a few days after that. But a full recovery really. I was back working two months later. With our friend Charles Raynor still in charge, can you believe?"

"I'm not surprised. That fucking arsehole nearly killed both of us."

"Raynor has been sacked…or removed since though. They had a dropped bell on the ship about six months later, surprise surprise, and both divers were injured. Physical injuries are more difficult to deny, unlike ours."

"Yeah, that's true."

"So he's back out in the job market somewhere."

"Christ. He'll probably find something too! God help where ever that is. But he was out there when you went back to work, you say?

"Ja. And the doctor he left the ship with to go bar crawling, as if nothing had ever happened. Still an arsehole. The diving went OK the next time, but I spent the whole decompression run with memories flooding back, waiting to pass out or feel the paralysis start again. Hated it, so I'm supervising now."

"Shit. Doc King says I'm medically unfit to do the deep stuff now. And I don't trust myself to supervise a team of four or six hairy-arsed divers. Or not yet anyway," Brian said.

"Oh shit. Maybe you should reconsider. I've worked with supervisors who couldn't read. Another one was deaf as a post and only used to pass his medical by lip-reading the doctor! It's official then with Doc King?"

"Well, sort of. Yeah. I did a fair bit of hyperbaric stuff down in Portsmouth. In a chamber at about 30 feet a few times a week. And scans and tests and bollocks. I've felt a bit better recently so I've been keeping busy doing some shallow inland or coastal stuff. That reminds me, I have to invoice for a job last week. Although, if I leave it, maybe they won't ask me back again," Brian agreed with himself, and promptly crossed out his written reminder. "Money was shit anyway."

"Probably always will be, once you get used to earning offshore bucks."

"I've got a job booked for a mate just after Christmas in the docklands up in London."

"Shit, man. Apart from having a catch up with my old diving partner, I was ringing with an offer for you. But now

I hear it from the horse's mouth, it doesn't sound like you'll be able to do it?"

"What's that, Mally?"

"It's a salvage job, Brian. But a deep one. Thirty-two gold bars at about 900 feet. Probably about a three to four-week round trip from port."

Brian's mood suddenly improved on hearing this most mouth-watering of projects. "No harm in telling me more is there?"

"Well, it's a "no cure, no pay" arrangement, so that ruled me out for a start. So I thought of you, as I know you know your stuff and probably have a few months left on your diving ticket? If you haven't already renewed it?"

"Yeah, it runs out middle of next year I think."

"It's a follow up job to clear up the remaining gold they couldn't salvage a couple of years back."

"Hmmm, pray tell," Brian said, feeling his health and medical ability to dive restored with every word, in his own mind at least.

"They know where the wreck is and there's no blasting through the hull to be done. That was all completed during the first job. There is my place available, but I can't do it on those terms. I've met the investor in Holland when I was last up for my course. A Dutch guy."

"Go on," Brian said, as he picked up a pen and pulled a notepad across the table. His fondness for hazardous pastimes such as this would be an aggravating factor to his retirement. He had had no time to switch on the radio on his stacker stereo system as he ran for the phone, so the damped scratching of the pen nib combined with his questions in the otherwise silent apartment. "You know you're tempting me here, don't you?"

"It's a World War Two wreck that went down with about 200 bars on board. Some kind of secret cargo. The first operation picked up about 160 of them before the weather closed in for the season."

"Season? Where is it, Mally?"

"The Barents Sea."

"Sounds cold?"

"Ja. About halfway to Russia from where you're sitting. Just up off the top of Norway."

"Why the delay then? Why didn't they go back the next season?"

"The gold price took a big dip soon afterwards so the profits would have been lower." Brian knew this to be the case, having scanned many recent commodity indexes for the price of silver. "But it's picking up again now. That and they made a huge pile of cash out of the first job."

"What's the deal with the Dutch guy. Investor?" Brian was doing his best, along with scribbled notes to absorb the overload of information Malcolm was sharing.

"Ja. You would have to go and meet him like I had to. A guy called Sebastiaan. Sebastiaan De Jonge is his name. He's heading some sort of consortium."

"Where, Mally?"

"He lives in Zandvoort, on the coast near Amsterdam. Where they do the Grand Prix, you know?"

"Oh, right. OK. I think I know the place."

"The usual bunch of rich idiots looking for some adventure by default, using us divers."

"Yep, I know the type. Met a few of those before. Bit of a pillock is he?"

"Big time."

"Met a few of those in my time as well."

"All I know about the job is that it will go ahead early next year, once the ice sheet retreats over the wreck. Er, what else? It's a four diver team, so three other guys in a small saturation system, don't know any names, based out of Peterhead."

"Can I think about it for a few days, Mally?"

"No problem. I haven't told him yet but I could introduce you in my place. If you change your mind that is, although it sounds made up already?"

"Ha ha. I'll let you know. Magic, nice to hear from you Mally. And Happy Christmas. I nearly forgot."

"Ja, Brian. Happy Christmas to you too china."

After the call ended, the details about where and when to meet Swiss Christian were two pages back in the notebook, as Brian had taken so many notes. He stood up, tightened the belt of his robe and headed to his kitchen to make a cup of tea. Malcolm had planted a seed. Brian just had to find a reason to resist. However, his fatalistic approach to life made it difficult to refuse an opportunity that he would otherwise leap naked through burning hoops for. He knew of similar salvage jobs and the associated rewards enjoyed by those who had done the work. As he stirred the milk into his agreeably brewed tea and brushed at his moustache, there was just one thing standing in his way agreeing to take Malcolm's place – something beyond the realm of money: his health.

08. Bicycle Basin

"Is diver on the bottom yet?" asked the gruff cockney voice of an east Londoner.

"Yep, on the bottom. Five fathoms down. Can't see a bloody thing though," Brian said.

"Just keep the wall to your right and walk forward to the corner about 50 feet and you should be there, Brian."

"That's easier said than done, so bear with me. I forgot how bad the visibility was in here. Christ."

"It's not great is it?"

"No it isn't." The docks' diving supervisor read the diver's path from his position by the white columns of air Brian released that fizzed like champagne bubbles as they surfaced. "Can you feed down some more line, please? It's feeling tight. You got some slack up there, yeah?"

The supervisor was next to the coil of bound pipes and cables and fed them down as the resistance grew on the umbilical, enough to demand more through his expert grasp. It was a twisted three-part hose of varying colour codes. Air was pumped down the yellow pipe, twice the bore of both the red communications cable and black pneumo hose for monitoring the diver's depth from the surface.

"Yep, all good up here. It must be caught down there. It happens a lot, as you can see."

"OK, give the line a good flick. If that don't work, I'll have to go back and find what the bloody thing is caught around."

A mighty tug with both hands, sufficient to either pull Brian over or tighten the umbilical around whatever it had snagged, did not free the diver.

"No good. Still won't budge. I'll have to go back and free it."

"OK, diver."

The supervisor listened with some amusement as Brian chuntered to himself while he traced back along the length of his umbilical.

"It might be an idea to follow me along the edge and feed it down to me that way afterwards. There's so much shit down here for it to snag on, it will probably happen again otherwise. Right, I've got it. It's caught around some bloody pipes. Please take up the slack. Yeah, that's good, that's enough," Brian guided the supervisor as he moved the unnecessary slack behind him to maintain the more direct feed Brian needed.

"Nearly there," Brian relayed. The effort in doing so dotted his speech with groans and grumbles over the intercom. Then the line went quiet, with just the infrequent static crackle feeding into the ears of Brian and the diving supervisor, who was sitting up on the quayside. Brian was 30 feet under the surface, traversing all manner of strewn items as he rummaged his way along the lower section of the quay.

"Are you in position, Brian?" A few seconds passed before the question was repeated. "Brian, are you in position now?"

"Oh bollocks, not a-bloody-gain," came the unhelpful reply.

"Everything OK down there, Brian?"

"Not quite, no. I'm where I should be now, I think."

The supervisor pre-empted Brian's next sentence, "But what? Are you caught up again?"

"No."

"Good. What's the problem?"

"I'm not down here alone, I'm afraid?"

"Eh? What d'you mean Brian?"

"Exactly that. I'm not down here alone," Brian said, sounding more certain than before.

"What d'you mean? You got a fucking mermaid after you or something?"

"I bloody wish."

"Well, you're the only diver we've got down there."

Brian was aware of that. His fellow bottom dweller had already been down there for a day or two and didn't require a secondary supply of air. However, as Brian palpated the object he had tripped upon, he could feel two spoked wheels and a bicycle frame. It was too heavy for him to move it away from his work area. Visionless in the inner-city broth of the dock basin, Brian's hands warily read the detritus, grope by grope. What felt suspiciously like arms that had been crudely bound to the frame, hands to the grips of the downturned handlebars shaped like cow horns and shoes attached to either pedal.

"I've got a body down here with me. Tied to a bloody bike I think."

"Are you sure?"

"You're welcome to come down here with me and double check if you want?"

Not thrown by a discovery that was not an uncommon occurrence in a city in excess of six million people, the supervisor's priorities were exposed, no matter how informed of protocol he was. "Can you move it out your way to get the job done, Brian?"

"No chance on my own. He's a heavy *baastard*."

"Roger. Please stay put while I organise a crane driver up here to pull the bugger up. If we can't continue, you're currently standing in a crime scene there, Brian."

"Oh, magic."

"I'll have to call the docks' old bill from the office when we get him out too."

The discovery capped a bittersweet return to the scene of the genesis of Brian's diving career, 14 years after he had greatly overstated his experience to be given his chance. It had been a vocation discovered relatively late in life that soon whisked him off around the globe and paid for his Maserati and boat, *Highroller* in short order. The seas and oceans of the world were his finishing school thereafter, what with the ever-increasing and much sought-after experience charted in his dive logbooks. Brian had more modern equipment at his disposal than he had had back in 1970 and now knew how it functioned. No more spherical brass helmets or the rubberised suits that Brian had no clue how to correctly inflate for buoyancy. The pumps providing the air through his umbilical line were powered by a generator, not two chain-smoking dive attendants. Lead-soled boots had been superseded by wellington boots, sealed around his shins with gaffer tape.

Great change had also occurred over the preceding years on a wharf within the same basin where Brian had first recovered copper coils dropped overboard while being unloaded. There was plenty of evidence of the "can-do" capitalist culture emerging after the relatively socialist post-war decades. Among the post-industrial landscape, most, if not all of the tri-legged cranes along either side of the once-bustling basin were pointed skywards and motionless. The bays beneath, with rounded edging stones were vacant, apart from piles of rigging slings and chains. Vaulted warehouses with windows on each floor supporting an arching lintel of bricks, built to store wool, tea and other prized goods hoisted from trading ships, were either empty or gutted. Where stevedores like Brian's uncles had once congregated along the crude drop-chain balustrading, now construction workers milled in the process of demolishing or repurposing the warehouses into apartments for the young upwardly mobile set. Hard hats had replaced the flat caps of the registered dock workers, at the behest of property speculators. Any sounds generated above the volume of speech rang around the docks with an arena-like echo.

He was a stone's throw from the swooping span of Tower Bridge and the Tower of London; the north and south towers of the grand river crossing were both visible as the derelict wharf that had blocked the view was razed to the ground. An acrid bonfire filled the otherwise fenced-off site behind where Brian was standing, with misty smoke, reluctant to disperse on that biting, windless morning. The docks had seen a steady decline since the mid-seventies, a decade that had ushered in automation, containerisation and ship designs in excess of the workable dimensions the dock on the north bank of the Thames could accommodate, if they were even able to reach it.

Brian's new inspection task should have been simple. However, a crisp December morning's work checking sluice gates, during the commercial lull between Christmas and New Year had become complicated almost immediately after he had got in the water. Brian's career regression, through no fault of his own, had never felt more acute than when the body emerged from the water on the end of a crane hook, still bound fast to the bike. Its front wheel spun lamentably as the figure was dropped onto the cobblestones behind a van that had brought all the diving equipment to site. The supervisor's battery radio was switched off in short-lived memoriam, just as the opening bars of "Careless Whisper" began to play.

Water continued to drain from the remains as it came to rest on its side, across a set of sunken tracks from a long disused bogey railway. Brian volunteered to detach the hook from the frame and provide a thumbs up to the operator. It was obvious the victim, fully clothed in a green bomber jacket and denims, and stiff as a sheet of marine plywood, could not have been an innocent passer-by. It would have been impossible to attach each limb to the corresponding handle or pedal without the "assistance" of several paid goons. Whoever he had angered, whether wilfully or otherwise, was the wrong person to provoke.

"He's either upset someone or that's a fucking weird hobby," the supervisor observed with a base Cockney humour that made the gallows variety seem light-hearted in comparison. In the surreal situation, Brian could not stifle a guilty laugh. "Poor bugger. What a way to go, eh? Being tied to that and then pushed off 'ere," the supervisor remarked and shook his head.

They both viewed the victim, who didn't look more than 20 years old. There was a long wait between alerting the police and their arrival. During the law enforcement vacuum caused by the delay, the supervisor's thoughts shifted to a gainful, amoral nature

"Eighteen gears. Metallic paint. Quite a nice racer, that. Hasn't been in there long. Bit of oil and a wipe, be good as new," he said shiftily to Brian as he fumbled for a penknife in the chest pocket of his jacket, intended to start cutting through the cord lashing the victim's hands to the drop handlebars. He clearly had a belated Christmas gift in mind.

"Do you want it? You found it?"

Brian politely refused the gentlemanly offer and watched as, without a shred of shame or remorse, the supervisor set about stealing an almost certainly pilfered bike from a dead man, before the police arrived.

"No, you be my guest."

"You sure? Finders keepers and all that," the supervisor offered, in an ironic attempt at civility.

"I insist."

"GO ON, HOP IT!" the supervisor shouted at a group of local youths drawn to the recovery of the underwater cyclist, not keen on upping the number of witnesses to his impending offence.

Dock police officers estimated a tit-for-tat gangland murder connection and completely swallowed the familiar supervisor's explanation that the bike had detached from the victim during the lift. Which meant that it was absolutely not concealed under diving umbilicals, behind the locked rear doors of his works van. The remains of the hapless victim had to be tilted at an angle when being transferred into a blacked-out coroners' van, due to post-mortem stiffness, so it looked like he was still riding an invisible bike.

Brian's initial steps in returning to the workplace felt like restarting his career all over again with an unknown face or reputation. He could get offshore work, well-paid and involving weeks off in-between shifts, by making a phone call or two. But his efforts to move inshore only saw him picking up work others had more than likely refused. The only advantage was a return to your own bed each night, rather than a bunk beneath a snoring fellow diver in a pressurised tube, just wide enough to stand up in. He had paid his diving dues a long time before, so felt it would be difficult to motivate himself to continue to climb another career ladder he had already reached the peak of before his decompression sickness. How many more bodies would he have to fish out before the type of work would improve?

Much more of that and Malcolm's offer of Brian taking his spot in a team of salvage divers would start looking more plausible, despite the thoughts of Doc King. The trap had been baited.

09. Going Dutch

Brian had already packed his luggage, adhering to his instinctive maxim, "get packed when it's quiet". He was still convinced he could back out at any moment. This was despite the evidence of the shiny and scarred passport pushed under the cream handle of his ribbed suitcase. Until Swiss Christian reported back and the proceeds materialised, Brian was technically still skint. As long as his accountant remained out of the clutches of an ever-widening net of defrauded clients, Brian had zero liquidity and even less choice about the freshwater work he could afford to turn down. He was still loath to invoice for either of his on-shore forays, for fear of being invited back to perform more unpleasantness.

Such was the nature of an industry too used to losing colleagues, those who remembered him, or had worked with Brian were probably also aware of his incident; in the same way Malcolm had come to learn of the successful legal action Brian had pursued with terrier-like tenacity in Rio. Following a near two-year sabbatical from commercial diving, Brian's circle of peers had shrivelled. Offers like Malcolm's arose rarely during a normal working life. So, to receive such an enticing proposal just when he thought his own deep diving life had ceased, was tempting. Too tempting.

He called Malcolm and accepted the offer. "Well, Brian the body snatcher. I'll pass the message on for you and please... just one bit of advice, don't fuck it up!"

He left for Gatwick Airport to take a brief flight to Amsterdam with Malcolm's parting advice drumming around his head. Although Malcolm knew Brian probably wouldn't "fuck it up", there was no better judge of Brian's abilities. If things didn't go well, he faced a working future that would serve to reinforce the nickname Malcolm had just bequeathed his former diving partner. So what did he have to lose? All things considered, Brian's recent career reprisal offered a reassuring measure of progress, and this had been reinforced by Malcolm's account of his own return to work in Brazil. In spite of the terror of the decompression that awaited Malcom as the finale of his hitch, he was alive and well. The only reason for his move into supervising was his psychological, not physiological scars. But Malcolm had not been affected to the same degree as him. Brian's only physical scar was his crocked index finger from an accident in the North Sea.

Brian had never visited Zandvoort before. Any urge for a trip to the bleak seaside town had been low when all the illicit options in Amsterdam were available just beyond the reception of his hotel. He exited Zandvoort train station, which sat proud of a natural rise above the town, and reminded himself not to make a return visit. A bitter gale hit him forcing a zipping up of his leather jacket. Having managed beach resorts around Athens while married to his now-estranged Greek wife, Brian had developed a partiality for warm Mediterranean climes. However, a beach bar overlooking the North Sea in December wasn't a taste he had yet acquired. Resort Nautique wasn't a solo operation; there were what looked like hundreds more along the immediate sweeping coastline. Stretching as far as Brian could see to the north and south were beach-club style resorts in a setting more associated with the Baltic coast.

His stride was hindered by howling onshore gusts as he walked down the stairs from the promenade, aiming for the navy blue and white Resort Nautique sign. The sea churned and bubbled through sets of shallow waves that slowly rolled up the broad beach. Brian reached a long pavilion-like structure painted in similar colours, including the ramped roof that sloped down towards an entirely glazed front facing the beach. Imaginatively repurposed from what appeared to be a disused fish-processing unit, the empty outside deck had a footprint three times that of the restaurant building. A small plunge pool at its centre was pea green with algae. Around its edge were wooden sun-loungers or tables and chairs, arranged with Germanic precision. Marking the perimeter, below in the sand, Resort Nautique flags fluttered like fishtails at the top of tall poles. Inside the club, the interior designer had created a Floridian cruise-ship feel, bound for the Bahamas.

While Brian waited to be served a warming cognac at the bar, he noticed that everything was painted white: the bar along the rear of the restaurant on which he rested, the floor, any wall that wasn't glass, the roof and support struts, even the furniture. The only addition to the colour palate were the indigo cushions, both seat and backrests and tangerine scatter pillows on the sturdy sofas or peacock chairs. That's not to mention the illuminated Christmas tree Brian passed as he entered – a temporary splash of non-nautical festive colour.

Pre-warned to be on the lookout for a "pillock" that could always be found there, he asked the tall barman for an introduction as he poured Brian's beverage. "I'm here to see Sebastian, or Sebastiaan I should say? Is he here?" Brian had to speak loudly to be heard over a Meatloaf song playing.

"Ja, Mr De Jonge is over there," the barman replied, while helpfully pointing Brian in the correct direction with his eyes. Brian followed the stare to an area on the far side of the bar from the entrance, secreted away from initial view. There he saw a tall, surly-looking man with a hooked nose overhanging a set of undulating fish lips and a broad, pointed chin. His hair was mousy brown, curls thick with gel, and his eyes dark blue and devious. Mr De Jonge wore a tight purple t-shirt under a shoulder-padded ivory jacket, left unfastened to the waist, paired with chalky white trousers. The fibres of his jacket shone cheaply when caught in the low blinding sun, which was pinned above the horizon out to sea. His Miami Vice tribute was completed by a pair of espadrilles and bare, sockless ankles – a plucky choice given the weather. Thankfully for Brian, he wasn't in Zandvoort to make new friends, so he could engage with someone he would normally avoid. Every salvage project needed a wealthy idiot to finance it, and Brian was meeting the latest in a long line for endorsement.

"Sebastiaan?"

"*Yesh*," he replied with a profuse Dutch accent.

"I'm Brian Worley, a colleague of Malcolm's. Pleased to meet you," Brian lied as he offered his hand in greeting. In reply, he received an overly firm handshake above Sebastiaan's table before pulling out the chair opposite. Between the disturbed cutlery, besides a pair of turbo sunglasses, was a mobile phone on full display. The handset connected through a spiral cable to the battery pack, that Brian estimated was similar in size and weight to the one in his car.

"*Yesh* Brian, I've been *exshpecting* you. Please call me Bas."

"Ok, Bas. Your choice. May I join you?"

"*Yesh*, you are welcome."

"Magic." Brian placed his cognac on the tablecloth before dragging the chair back under himself. Closer in, the fumes of Kouros aftershave emitting off Bas displaced the general aroma of food preparation Brian had been smelling since his arrival.

Bas was slouched against one side of his chair, his elbow rested on his locked legs. He swung his expensive watch around with a clenched fist to check the time, in a show that he too was a man of a world and time was money. But his guest read this as further proof, were it needed, that he was about to initiate discussions on a salvage deal with a complete prick. The deeply tanned chest in mid-winter and flawless, polished fingernails spoke of a man more familiar with carrot tanning oil and nail technicians than the ocean floor.

"You're British right, Brian?" Bass probed, with usual Dutch frankness.

"Yep," Brian confirmed, meeting Bas's stare after settling into his chair. "Cheers. Good to meet you too Bas."

"*Cheersh*. So you want to *replashe* Malcolm on our little job?"

"Maybe, but that's why I'm here."

"OK, so he told you it's in the Barents Sea, *yesh*?"

"He did?"

"Off the Norwegian coast?"

"That too."

"Did he tell you the story about the sinking?"

"No, we only had a brief call. I know most of the gold has been recovered already. That's about it."

"*Yesh*. And we go back for the rest. So I offer you the same terms as Malcolm. No cure, no pay you say?"

"Yep, that's right. I know that. I get nothing if we don't salvage anything."

"*Yesh*, correct."

"And if all goes well though? Then what?"

"You'll get ten percent of the profits. Shared between the divers."

"Ten percent of what?" Brian asked, taking his turn to be frank.

"Thirty-two gold bars remain down there. Loaded onto a merchant ship so the wreck isn't classed as a war grave. There was a salvage job two *yearsh* ago which cleared up much of it. Thirty-two times ten kilo bars is 320 kilos of gold. And 350 ounces per bar works out at today's price at $111,000 per bar. So about three and a half million dollars in gold in total. And we just go and get the rest."

"You make it sound easy, Bas."

"Easier for me, as I don't go down and get the stuff. If this goes well, our consortium will do other jobs. Do you know how much war gold that left port actually reached its destination?"

Brian didn't and preferred to keep to the subject at hand. "No I don't. Probably not much?"

"It was 34 percent. So 66 percent is still down there, can you believe that, just waiting for guys like us. Unbelievable!"

Brian bristled internally at Bas's assumption of any likeness between the two of them – they were just two sides of a symbiotic relationship in which neither could achieve the fantastical outcomes alone.

"So roughly $350,000 between four divers?"

"*Yesh.*"

Brian's chin extended while he pulled his right eye closed to perform mental arithmetic, "So halve that, and half again. About 87 grand each, roughly?"

"*Yesh*, about that."

"Is that all?" Brian said, as a tongue-in-cheek aside.

Bas proved he had neither a tongue nor cheek and replied sharply, "Your colleagues were happy to accept. And we don't even have to find it: just sail back out there to it."

"I was only pulling your leg, Bas."

"I'll provide the boat, the helium and oxygen *gash* and diving gear for the job, all the crew and accommodation in Scotland before you leave."

Brian thought it best not to enquire about the source of Bas's wealth and that of his fellow investors. "Where in Scotland, Bas?"

"Petershead, I think it's called. Or Peterhead? All the important things are set up, so anything else happens now, like Malcolm pulling out, is just a "child's disease", as we say in Dutch."

Brian glossed over what seemed a very odd expression to describe niggling yet surmountable obstacles and continued some final detailed questions, consistent with a man who wanted in. "So four divers. Malcolm told me he came to meet you, have you met the others?"

"*Yesh*, of course. I had to make sure they were people I could do business with, just like you are, Brian," Bas appeared to like his adventurous guest, a feeling totally unrequited by Brian. "There are two more Englishmen – Michael and Roy. And a younger Canadian called Tim. All with North Sea experience. Good guys."

"Do you know any surnames?" Brian asked, hoping to place them rather than rely on Bas's judgement.

Bas shook his head, "I'll have to look those up for you, Brian."

"No don't worry. I was just curious if I knew them. When do you think this will happen, Bas?

"We think about two months from now. At the beginning of March. You have a fax machine?"

"Yes."

"*Pleash* leave your number and I'll fax you details nearer the time. But no contract. This is a handshake-only deal. I only work on handshakes. That is my bond."

"No problem," Brian concurred, mindful to check how many fingers remained when they shook on the deal, over their Chicken Kiev and plate of fried whitebait, respectively.

A flick of Bas's hand resulted in a bottle of champagne in a frosted ice bucket being brought to their table, two saucer-shaped coupes frothed as they were generously filled. In consummation of their informal arrangement, Bas cockily lifted his glass by the thin stem in his manicured hand and toasted, "Brian, Here's to a successful 1985."

"Cheers. Happy New Year. Magic," Brian concurred as their glasses met.

"Yesh. And here's to mixing business with *treashure*."

10. The Navy Tot

"If Hitler, or anyone else for that matter, wanted to attack us, they should've waited until after eleven o'clock in the morning, son. That's when the daily rum ration was given out; the whole navy was drunk by midday." Arthur said this about the Navy tradition, describing the daily ration of rum issued to all seafaring men, known as the "tot".

They were the first words Arthur Peacock had ever uttered about his wartime naval career. This was 37 years after the celebrations of V.E. Day, the preface to which were the Normandy landings on the beaches of Northern France. He was sitting in a swim with his grandson on a fishing lake he had joined since retiring. A link back to his past life of fishing the Thames in the East End as a child. Arthur was a cockney by birth who had settled and raised a family in Portsmouth on the south coast after the war. It was the naval port town from which he had first entered the services as a conscripted cadet, with only very basic seamanship training.

His first words about the war weren't to his children or doting wife, Gladys. Nor were they shared with his parents. His mother had lived on for 25 years after the war, reaching the age of 76. Her prime of life had been sandwiched between the world wars. His father, sadly, had been killed in the latter stages of the London Blitz, a year before Arthur set sail from Portsmouth for Murmansk on H.M.S. *Hawston*. All seemed exciting and spirits were raised when their chance came to take on

"Jerry" out on the open sea, for King and country. During a treacherous voyage through the Arctic Oceans, a journey Winston Churchill rightly dubbed "the deadliest of them all". Arthur would soon discover just how accurate an assessment that was.

His accepted silence on the matter was never questioned or challenged. Surviving photos of Arthur in naval uniform had long since been packed and put away in the loft, never again to see the light of day. He was from a generation drafted to fight the tyranny of the Nazi regime, so those that followed could be spared the horrors that Arthur and others had witnessed. They never spoke of their involvement. Not at a family dinner or Christmas gatherings or summer holidays. He might have profited from his knowledge when various individuals connected to the first gold salvage had sought him out. But he had turned down their repeated overtures to participate, two years earlier in 1982. Many of that generation would take their experiences to the grave, rather than revisit them every time somebody asked a question. Nevertheless, Arthur wanted somebody to know something of what he had gone through, even if it was a sanitised account for the benefit of younger ears. His grandson, Kevin, was a freckled faced ten-year-old who liked Star Wars films and BMX bikes.

Arthur was 67 years old in the spring of 1985, six months' shy of his next birthday and retired. Now portly with thinning silver hair, his perspective on life had shifted in his twilight years. Soon he would be gone himself. Rather than just fading into elderly obscurity, shunned as a pension-drawing irrelevance by younger people living fast-paced lives, he wanted someone to know what he had buried deep inside him his whole life. Memories that had troubled him every single day since, sunken as deep as the gold he had been charged to guard. This included the amazing story of how he had survived the sinking of the merchant ship, *The Perseverance*, in the Barents Sea.

In June 1942, he disembarked from H.M.S. *Hawston* at the port of Murmansk, 25 miles upstream from the mouth of the Kola River, which emptied into Kola Bay of the Barents Sea. The passage through the deep channel feeding into the bay was tense and edifying. No basic training could in any way prepare a raw recruit for the appalling sights, sounds and smells of war they would encounter even before they left the ship. The night before they entered the Kola channel, 12,000 bombs had been dumped on the port and city. Built largely of wooden dwellings, the city had been spared the attentions of the German war machine until then. Reporting massive loss of life with minimal military losses, the scene hours later at daybreak under a lead-grey birdless sky was one of utter devastation. As H.M.S. *Hawston* sailed past northern stretches of the city, the landscape was just a smouldering sea, awash with double-storey chimney stacks, the only structures not to have been incinerated. The smell of burnt timber and flesh carried in bitter winds was thick in the air, and the bloated bodies of the population in the water were too numerous to count. The bombing was in response to stubborn Russian resistance to Operation Barbarossa, the German invasion of their former ally on its eastern front. It was an attempt to shift focus away from the south of Russia, to attack one of few ports that was ice-free year round. It would remain a critical Allied port for as long as Moscow held the territory. A quarter of all military aid was being funnelled through the docks, and payments in gold sailed regularly in the opposite direction. So the Germans were intent on disabling this Allied back door into Russia.

After docking and probably entering early-stage shock himself, Arthur saw a panicked, chaotic scene in the gigantic port. American tanks and planes were being offloaded on one quay. On the next, shells the size of children were being rolled off ships on planks like barrels of wine. Long-coated Russian soldiers, each with a rifle hung from a shoulder by a leather strap, fraternised with nervous sailors wearing back-tailed navy dress. Even the hardened dockers looked jumpy as the anti-aircraft sirens sounded and guns fired salvos up into the sky. Shipbuilding yards were frantically repairing some ships and constructing others, in attempts to outpace the German fleet of U-boats' capacity to sink as many as possible. The tactic of downing even merchant ships in significant numbers to cripple the supply lines was beginning to bite both Russia and her Allies. The Lend & Lease act – the requisition of merchant vessels by the Navy to meet the demands of the war effort – had brought *The Perseverance* into service. The steam passenger liner, given over to the naval campaign, had transported telephone cable, boots, blankets, cotton and nylon for the manufacture of webbing to Murmansk.

Pockets of local civilians ambled around the harbour in downright desperation presumably having been bombed from their homes the previous night. There were families, old couples, and orphaned children. Some were walking wounded with bandages wrapped around body parts and caked in dried blood. The corpses of those who had succumbed to their injuries lay where they had fallen.

Under that were trodden once prized possessions, jewellery and valuables, in the mud and worthless. Others just wandered lost and aimless, their spirit broken. They carried what remained of their worldly assets, recovered from their burning houses: dogs, cats, heirlooms, bicycles, carriage clocks and wheelbarrows. Arthur would remember their cries the most; they were branded into his memory. The complete loss of hope gave rise to wails and screams, all wholly disturbing for someone just off a ship at his first harbour in a conflict zone. Arthur would not continue on with the H.M.S. *Hawston*. Fortune appeared to be smiling on him when he received sudden orders to decamp onto *The Perseverance* for an immediate voyage back to Blighty, along with a fellow new recruit.

Two navy guards were needed to watch a shipment of 20 mysterious wooden boxes, each wound in fresh copper twine. Arthur was chosen by chance in the chaos, with another cadet who couldn't have been older than 20 years old. He was called Kenneth, a young man who was constantly pushing his spectacles back onto his face. He had terrified eyes that darted around in their sockets and was visibly more affected by the scene than Arthur. So Arthur guided his greener charge over to *The Perseverance*, past rows of anti-tank guns and beneath patrolling Russian jets that flew so low over the port, Arthur felt he could have reached up and touched them. In his pale blue frock coat and saluting to anyone they encountered around *The Perseverance*, the two young naval guards were soon aboard and happy to have scored a swift passage out of such a diabolical setting. Apart from the boxes, the ship was mainly carrying the more severely injured naval personnel back for medical treatment.

Seaman Arthur Peacock felt fortunate as he and young Kenneth departed Murmansk just 14 hours after arriving. The younger of the two was given the first 12 hours of guard duties, and posted in the corridor opposite the doorway to the room where the boxes had been hastily stored before departure. Unsettled and terrified, Arthur stood on the upper deck of *The Perseverance*, chain-smoking filterless Woodbines. He was especially tense as the ship retraced the channel out to sea. A more seasoned crew member on portside deck-watch came and shared Arthur's cigarette, and filled in the blanks as to the nature of his mission. All the military hardware Arthur had viewed in Murmansk had to be paid for. The debt due to the British or Americans was being settled from Russian gold reserves amassed deep underground in Muscovite vaults. But repayments didn't always reach their destination, such was the success of interceptions by the U-Boat fleet. Much to the embarrassment of a reeling Admiralty in London, 460 gold bars had been lost on an armoured destroyer only two months' earlier, complete with a full Arctic convoy sent as protection.

So the vital, valuable loads were being reduced and split across varying types of vessels, in an expensive exercise of trial and error. Some were even travelling without a convoy, as the Germans had gotten wise to such ship formations being used to protect something valuable. Other times, decoy convoys were used to draw the focus of enemy submarines from specific merchant ships, such as *The Perseverance*. Sailing on a liner carrying less than half the load lost on the destroyer, Arthur's tension began to lift with the opening of the channel out into the bay. He felt something approaching reassurance entering a larger sea, and crossing into north Norwegian waters. A floating needle in a haystack, sailing choppy waters that were more white horse than ocean. The Barents Sea looked most deserving of its ferocious reputation, which Arthur had seen vindicated on his outward voyage.

Under the midnight sun and with only three seconds of a screamed warning from the starboard lookout, following the audible blow of an object striking the hull, a submerged mine blew apart the rear of *The Perseverance*. Once the initial shock faded, the Captain felt the bow of his ship lift as the ruptured stern took on water. Young Kenneth, stationed at his post below the waterline, was engulfed in the rising water as it inundated the split compartments of the ship. Mayday calls were sent out and life rafts lowered; they struck the sides of the heeling hull as they neared the water. Those onboard who were still able to walk, or crawl in some cases, made it up onto deck. The more seriously injured or less mobile would go down with the stricken ship.

The Perseverance was still afloat for a further two hours. The angle of the decks from bow to stern dropped some thirty degrees. This was enough to warrant ropes being tethered and dropped down the timber decking to climb up from the stern. The steam engines were snuffed out and silent, *The Perseverance* owed its remaining service to the currents that spun it in circles as it sank deeper. Arthur, seeing the operational lifeboats already full with injured servicemen much more in need than himself, buttoned up his woollen coat and leapt from the side. The temperature of the sea made his body rigid on entry. All around him cries for help could be heard as he kept his arms spinning through the water, as much to keep his circulation going as to swim for a timber sheet tossed overboard.

A Norwegian fishing vessel responded first to the distress calls; its valiant crew rescued Arthur and eight others from the freezing sea. Two more sunk from view waiting for the small Norwegian craft to reach them as more fortunate survivors were pulled from the sea and wrapped in blankets. With ringing deafness in both ears, Arthur got a macabre front row seat watching the last throws of *The Perseverance*. Her bow was the last to disappear after the single oval funnel belched a final acrid cloud from up-rushing waters that loosened soot deposits as old as the ship.

Within ten minutes, the only trace was the shivering men rescued by the Norwegian fishermen, three lifeboats drifting with the current and an ever-expanding slick of oil. This created a strangely beautiful pool of rainbow colours to Arthur's traumatised eyes, as he sipped at a bottle of rum passed among the survivors.

And that was Arthur's story, recounted to his grandson on that bright spring morning as he passed young Kevin a new rod, ready to cast.

11. Showroom to Scotland

"But *Bri-yon*. If you want to, I *zink* you should do *zis*," Brian's fiancée Anne had said, much to his surprise during a reunion dinner in Marseille, in a show of matrimonial *Liberté, Egalité & Fraternité*. Brian hadn't been her first relationship with a professional diver so Anne knew how the industry worked and the inability of mad divers to refuse such projects. Maximillian and Claudette, his future father and mother-in-law, had joined Anne's young daughter Kathleen around the table to approve of the union with their favourite English daredevil. He was there to request their daughter's hand in marriage, but their beaming faces were all the consent Brian needed. They were the ones who had first questioned Anne about why she wasn't already involved with him when he first arrived at their home in Marseille in his Maserati.

With his finances unable to support a costly excursion to the French Rivera where the purchase of an engagement ring would be involved, Brian had to be a little evasive when providing a date for his visit once he had accepted Anne's long-standing proposal. That was before Brian had his hush-hush follow-up meeting with Swiss Christian, behind the circular art deco pavilion at the end of Worthing pier. Empty flagpoles were fixed at regular intervals around the structure, like points on a compass. Ornate lamps along the length of the pier illuminated the boardwalk planking. Christian obviously had an appreciation of Victorian follies, or the solitude they afforded for such consultations. On that morning in

January 1985, the winter sun rose reluctantly to the east against a dark ruby horizon. The low tide had withdrawn the flat surf back from the pebble beach, so almost half the pier's length rose up out of the exposed mud flats, which reflected the crimson rays. Brian's brown leather jacket was zipped tight and glowed a deep purple in the morning light. They were about 1,000 feet from the promenade, with a view from behind the waves marching to their end, short of the shore. Brian had been patient and was due for a pleasant, if very well earned surprise.

"I have good news *und* good news for you," Christian announced as a cryptic greeting, stood in a trench coat.

"Magic, that sounds good."

"*Vell*, it *vasn't* silver."

"That doesn't sound like good news?"

Christian saw the confusion spreading across his client's face. "It *vas* platinum."

Which clarified Brian's lingering question over the absence of silver sulphide deposits. "Oh, that explains why it was so clean."

"Ja, my buyer in Antwerp confirmed *ze* following. Fineness *vas* 98%. Current market price per ounce is $270 per ounce, times 70 in each bar. *Zis* makes £18,900 per bar. Times four is £75,600 in total. I take the £5,600 as commission, *vhich* leaves £70,000 for you. Enjoy it. Good day."

With that, Christian handed over the proceeds in a crinkled brown envelope before he spun on quarter-tipped heels and walked back to land. Brian stayed put and watched the unremarkable precious metal dealer blend back into the world unnoticed, before he followed. The *Dalhousie* had given up its biggest secret, which allowed Brian to recoup all of his outlay on the efforts to raise the entire ship, more or less. Barge charter and fit-out costs, paying Anne's cousin Lolly a retaining wage to research the wreck during Brian's enforced work schedule to finance it, not to mention his own time and energy - had all been reimbursed with interest. It all came down to a pile of unregistered, soiled sterling notes on his dining table where the bars had sat. There would be no glory of the find or first salvage of any East Indiaman ship. Just a few of the relics survived, like the copper clock bezel and what remained of the workings of the ship's rudder, in the spare room of his apartment. The wreck had just paid him back in spades for his persistence and Brian gladly cashed out his chips at the Channel casino. It was also enough for him to up the repayment of Bill's loan to £4,000 – a well-deserved doubling of his debt repayment.

On Brian's return to a bright and breezy Brunswick Square, a distorted message was waiting on his answering machine: "Morning Brian. It's Doc King. Sorry I missed you. Not sure if you know already, but our accountant friend has indeed been found. In the Philippines. So some good news to start the day... and bad for him, one presumes. Call me back when you get a chance, please."

Next to the answering machine was the fax machine, which had just spat out a much anticipated message, accompanied by a screeching telecoms tone and a climactic beep.

BOULEVARD BERNAARD

ZANDVOORT

2041 KE

HOLLAND

TEL: 003123740743

FAX: 003123740744

RESORT NAUTIQUE

Fax

COMMENTS:

CONDITIONS FAVOURABLE FOR MARCH. ASSEMBLE 01/03/1985 IN PETERHEAD PORT, SCOTLAND.

ACCOMMODATION IN WAVERLEY HOTEL BOOKED.

SHIP NAME - GALLOPER.

CHARTER DATES - 01/03/1985 TO 05/04/1985.

DIVERS NAMES - MICHAEL GOODBRAND, ROY IVES, TIM WINGEN, BRIAN WORLEY.

DIVE SUPERVISORS NAMES - SERGIO SOUZA, DAVIDE LAURENT.

DIVE SUPERINTENDENT NAME - GORDON CLARK.

SAIL ON 02/03/1985 - DIVING SYSTEM TO BE MOBILISED ON OUTWARD VOYAGE.

By the time everything was confirmed by Bas, Brian was financially flush, so had additional reason not to accept the job, despite Anne's insistence over their long lunch that he should. However, it would potentially be an illustrious bookend to his diving career. It had been two years since he last entered a pressurised saturation chamber and he had aged visibly in that time. Further grey hairs were crowding out his temples and moustache. His unease was rational, considering he and Malcolm had almost perished on their final shift. A return call with Doc King further clouded his decision.

"They found the arsehole, pardon my French."

"That's a bloody relief. That didn't take so long then."

"No it didn't. Good news, eh? Mrs King is most pleased I can assure you."

"Yeah, magic. Thanks for letting me know."

"My absolute pleasure, Brian."

"There might be a Mrs Worley soon, by the way."

"Blimey, are you sure you're feeling alright?"

"I feel OK. Doing much better. Sorry I missed your call Doc, I was out doing some business."

"I won't ask what that was concerning," Doc King said knowingly. This was partly for his own protection. "Apparently, you have two of your American co-workers to thank for this. They found him by bribing someone at Manila airport for his landing card and then applied the applicable amount of physical retribution upon his person, so to speak. We should see all our money back in our accounts this week; after that they'll release him."

"Shit. I wouldn't want to be in that *baastard's* shoes at the moment."

"No, me neither. I'm told he'll walk with a limp for the rest of his days."

"Magic!"

Doc King's response to Brian's news of the salvage offer was less than effusive.

"Well, I know I can't stop you. But, speaking in the capacity of your friend, I think you'd be entirely mad to even consider doing that and, as your physician, clinically insane to then go ahead with it. I could put it no plainer than that."

"When have you known me to be sane, Doc?"

"Good point, Brian. You have to be somewhat mad to do your job. I'm sure there's a potential payday involved somewhere?"

"Yeah, a share of 320 kilos of gold."

"Gordon Bennett! Even so. Why don't you just do that *Titanic* job you told me about? The video survey thing? Keeps you up out of the water where you belong now."

"I was keen until the accountant buggered off with our money. It's not really a direction I want to go in anyway."

"As your doctor again now, you know I wouldn't renew your diving certs on medical grounds."

"I know that, Doc."

Doc King knew, just like Anne, he might be wasting his breath, but continued for his own conscience more than Brian's, "Well, don't come crying to me if you end up in a wheelchair. But best of British luck to you anyway. See you, Brian." He placed the receiver back onto the phone in his surgery office and shook his head. Doc King had viewed sufficient scans of his patient's reworked brain to believe that might have been the last phone call he would receive from Brian.

As his monies were soon due to be restored, Brian flouted Bill's guidance to rejig his approach to monetary matters with a more responsible mind by visiting the nearest Porsche dealership. His experience of Ital-Franco engineering with his Maserati Merak had been both joyful and money-sapping with the constant cost of tuning or repairs. So next time around, he was going German. The pile of *Dalhousie* booty was burning a Porsche 928S-sized hole in his pocket. Assets were to be posed in, not lived in, he thought. Irrespective of how shocking the depreciation rate might prove when the time came to part with it.

"No problem, Mr Worley. We can organise that for you. And we can fit the car phone option prior to delivery, sir. Please follow me through to my office to sign on the dotted line." With a grin, Brian shook hands with the franchise salesman across the narrow sunroof of the show model's cabin. He had walked in intending to buy the classic 911, but had been seduced by the more modern car. A continent-crossing grand tourer, perfect for gobbling up the miles between his home in Brunswick Square and Anne's, in the south of France. The fact that the salesman happened to mention the 928S coupe had a higher top speed than the model Brian had originally wanted was the deal clincher. Delivery was due in mid-March after working his way up a waiting list, so the arrangements would have to be re-thought. He changed it from a simple showroom collection in Brighton to a quayside delivery in Peterhead and postponed it by two weeks. His theory was that his newest toy would be awaiting him once the salvage job had wound up.

Brian increased his visits to the local leisure centre in an attempt to strengthen his upper body and, in particular, his neck for the task ahead. He managed only half of a probable twelve hours he would need to complete a shift run on the salvage. Afterward, he had acute soreness in his shoulder and neck muscles, which would be supporting a 20-kilo helmet for the duration. He reacquainted himself with heliox gas mixture tables and decompression charts from documents found in the pockets of his briefcase. He skipped the final entry in Rio when reviewing his dive log books, not wanting the reminder. Despite a faulty memory, he hadn't forgotten much. Over the days and weeks until the salvage job began, he followed a similar routine to prepare to work offshore again.

Not a single member of his family knew of his troubles over the previous two years. He was certainly a less frequent visitor during what, to them, had appeared to be another work time-out, an extended one in this case. So an update on his next bite of life was neither necessary nor in his nature. Bill was the sole person he had confided in, outside of the industry that was drawing him back. Anne also knew and was strangely supportive, perhaps seeing that a favourable outcome to one last adventure would translate to an easier life for both. Perhaps they could afford the French beach bar they had spoken of before, an idea Brian had few reservations over, if any. If she had been privy to the medical reports and opinions of the respected hyperbaric specialists who had taken a decent poke around the inside of many a diver's skull, then perhaps her backing would not have been so forthcoming. Brian provided a sanitised version of events, so as not to spook his future in-laws into thinking Anne was marrying a walking, talking corpse, should he dive again.

The morning of 28th February started with multiple journeys in the wrought-iron lift from his fourth floor abode through the centre of a circular staircase feeding every floor. Duffle bags bursting with suits and helmets and a tan suitcase with winter clothes and footwear were loaded into his car boot. There were also some everyday clothes for some socialising pre-trip, and hopefully post-trip too. The balance was thick socks, jogging bottoms and woollen jumpers, his garb when not on shift, out in the wild depths in a heated neoprene suit. Folded between these were a carton of cigarettes, a bottle of good cognac and aniseed boiled sweets. The latter treat was permissible in a compression chamber, although pretty much tasteless once the pressure rose. A silk-lined, leather-effect case housed his Remington shaver set, a must for keeping his bristling moustache in order, slid into an open side pocket.

A 600-mile journey lay between him on the Brighton seafront and Peterhead in the Grampians in north-east

Scotland, beyond the Tartan Curtain. On a last visit upstairs, to double-check that he'd left nothing behind, Brian paused for a moment. He closed the drinks globe in the corner of his bay window and took in the view over the square from his apartment; a last look across the flat roofs separated by the shared chimney stacks and TV aerials of each townhouse. He quietly pulled his front door closed to the feint noise of his neighbour's hairdryer, as she prepared for another day at work. From a floor or two below, there was the sound of another neighbour leaving and locking his door. When the dreary working world outside his penthouse had little to offer Brian in terms of a career as fulfilling as diving had proven, it was simple to countenance a return to work under the deep blue sea.

12. Wee Four

Moments after glancing through a recent visitor's bill, Moira, a pretty, bespectacled receptionist at the Waverley Hotel, looked up to see a moustachioed guest with a rakish smirk approaching her. She began her arrival spiel once Brian reached the front desk. By the time it concluded, her guest had collapsed down onto his right knee, both arms out to his side like stabilisers. His breathing was short and shallow.

"Oh, are you OK sir?" Moira asked, frightened and unsure of what to say as his shoulder thumped against the panel under the front of her desk. Brian clearly wasn't OK. Stifled, frustrated groans signalled his discomfort and resistance to the sudden symptoms. He had eventually left Brighton early afternoon, the journey had taken longer than planned; 12 hours had turned into 17 with butterflies forever hatching in his stomach. It had also been elongated by a set of unforeseen roadworks, a blizzard and a food stop for an ostensibly fried breakfast at a Trusthouse Forte motorway services. He had felt fine throughout, perhaps somewhat drowsy back on the road after his bacon and eggs, but otherwise nothing to report. It had been weeks since his last migraine and his head had been free of pain that morning. But now his disobedient body was shuddering in a fit of incoherent muscle spasms. "Sir, let me help you," Moira announced reassuringly in her soft Aberdonian accent before shouting to her colleague,

"RHONA! COME HELP ME HERE!"

With some urgency, they both helped to stand Brian back up from his haunches. He was already showing improvements as they moved him into a chair they had pulled out from a back office. As he sat there, adjacent to the front desk, his left leg was the last area of his anatomy to keep trembling as he recovered, while stubbornly refusing any suggestions that an ambulance should be called. The restorative attention of the two attentive young ladies markedly revived Mr Worley. One of them even placed her phone number on the back of a hotel card, before pressing it into Brian's sweaty palm, seemingly with the unspoken offer of further comfort of a different nature should he require it. Ten minutes went by before Brian had returned to something like normal physically, and was back to his charming best. He gingerly pushed himself upright from the chair arms with a covering quip, "I don't think that haggis agreed with me, do you?"

In a room more befitting half the claimed four stars on the signage outside, Brian took to the bed. Deeply concerned and more than tired, he drifted off to sleep, baffled by what had just happened to him. He reflected on a long overnight drive on top of two months in which he had rested little, what with selling off the *Dalhousie* loot and a preparatory fitness routine. His efforts to re-energise what remained of his career onto a more lucrative footing must have taken a toll. He found no other reasonable explanation for why his central nervous system had gone haywire, no matter how sudden or brief it was. If a similar event had been repeated when he was outside a diving bell, he could only uncomfortably speculate what the outcome would be. So, after a siesta, he could either phone Doc King and report the fit, or blot it out as a one-off – then simply slip on a shirt and tie and go to self-medicate with cognac. If his fellow divers were also booked into the Waverley Hotel as the fax suggested, then at least one would be found in their natural habitat in the early afternoon – the hotel bar.

Apart from a couple sat on either side of the saloon awash with the Iberian sounds of Julio Iglesias, an urbane-looking man was enjoying a pint of lager. Fit and fresh, he had silver-blonde long, parted hair, pale eyebrows and lashes and stood six feet tall, a couple of inches taller than Brian. A pair of clean-shaven cheeks dimpled below elevated square cheekbones when he smiled.

"Are you Roy, Tim or Michael by any chance?" Brian asked, leaning over the same bar and flicking his head up to catch the barman's eye.

"Hello there, matey. Yes, I'm Michael. You must be Roy or Brian because Tim is Canadian, right?"

"Oh magic. I'm the Brian one."

"What can I get you, Brian?"

"A large cognac would be bloody magic please, Michael," Brian replied, heartened that at least one of the bodies he would share a compression chamber, or "pot" as they called it, for an unknown number of days, wasn't an arsehole. It seemed that the feeling was reciprocated by his new partner as they shook hands warmly.

"Are you OK? I saw you by the reception this morning when I arrived," Michael asked politely as the barman prepared his fresh order.

"Christ, yeah. Just had a funny turn I think," Brian bluffed at the unexpected question.

"Well, you look ship-shape and Bristol fashion now. Hope you are feeling better, matey," Michael raised his glass from the pool of overspill surrounding it, "Cheers, Brian. Good to meet you and here's to a successful job."

"Good health," Brian returned.

Over the course of their first beverage, Brian learned of Michael's passion for seeking out uncharted shipwrecks in his free time, when not manning the lifeboat from his local RNLI station. He lived on the coast in Great Yarmouth, the English cousin to Aberdeen as a hub for the offshore oil industry. He was a capable multi-tasking diver with a length of career comparable to Brian, with one big distinction – Michael had never had a decompression sickness. They hit it off well; Michael keyed into Brian's personality immediately. The next thirsty character to appear in the bar was tall and wiry, with slender forearms full of faded tattoos. A salt-blasted complexion was outlined by a deep, square chin and mischievous blue eyes. His greying hair was short and shaggy. With a butter-thick Devon accent carried on a gravel voice, he asked, "I'm guessing you're Michael and *Broin*?" and lifted both eyebrows, following his hunch. His eccentricities were yet to be revealed.

"That's right, matey," Michael said in greeting. "I'm Michael." Brian nodded and offered a handshake.

"Roy Ives, pleased to meet you both, boys."

"You want a drink, Roy?" Brian asked as he signalled to the barman with a grey five-pound note, folded lengthways between his thumb and forefinger.

"A beer'll do me, thanks, *Broin*."

For all Brian's reasonable trepidation, he couldn't have asked for better colleagues thus far. Roy was five years Brian's senior. A career of 20 years spent underwater had been just as diverse and well-travelled as Brian's. He had recently returned from working on a blown-out rig in the Gulf of Mexico with the infamous oil well firefighter, Red Adair. He also taught commercial diving courses in Fort Bovisand, below the waters of Plymouth Sound –which the ex-garrison was originally built to defend. Shaped and seasoned by the sea, Roy's maritime knowledge of almost every ship that had been lost off the coast of Plymouth was hands-on and encyclopaedic. His collection of recovered goods ranged from live ammunition, cannons, effects such as ships' plates and bells, clay pipes, bottles, amphoras, propellers, brass portholes, and even perfectly preserved leather aprons recovered from a Russian wreck. If something had sunk with a ship, then Roy would be interested in following it down and fetching it.

Tim, last to be drawn to the hotel bar; of the three reprobates chatting, recognised Brian immediately. He was 15 years Brian's junior, just a couple of years into his thirties, but they had almost worked alongside each other in the North Sea, some ten years' earlier. Transport in the form of a coach had been taking divers interested in a dicey job south of their Aberdeen base. Had the job not been too risky for Tim and financially rewarding enough to convince Brian, they would have worked together on that job. As tall as Roy, but broader of beam, Tim had downturned plate-eyes, the left fractionally lower than the right. He had a mop of brown hair with a twist on every end from his fringe over his ears to his nape, and a stubbly beard, which was thicker across his top lip.

"Brian? Brian Worley? Is that you?" Tim asked in his North American accent.

"Oh, bloody 'ell. Magic, nice to see you," Brian replied drawing his head back in recognition as he scrabbled around his mind to place the face.

"It's Tim. We nearly worked on that batshit crazy pipeline job at some gas terminal in Teesside." Tim was a fan of outdoors language; it peppered his speech like punctuation. He was a blunt man who wasn't afraid to call a spade a motherfucking spade.

"Oh, Jesus. That one."

"I didn't need the money that fucking badly."

"I bloody did. Nice to see you again. Still a scruff I see."

"You bet. Weren't you working on re-floating a sunken ferry in Libya or Algeria, or some fucking place?"

"That's right. Good memory Tim."

"How did that salvage work out?"

"It had sunk again by the time I got back down there after the rig," Brian said sideways to Tim with a grin above an extended jaw. He felt a duty to introduce him to the line-up. "Michael, Roy, say hello to Tim."

Sebastiaan may have had a hideous fashion sense and questionable taste in hotels, but his sheer luck in attracting four such capable aquanauts augured a swift and successful outcome. The drinks orders flowed, and were assigned to expenses via room numbers. The volume of the conversation rose, as the stock levels diminished, along with the patience of the barman serving them. The evening was young, the night even younger and their socialising skills yet to be truly measured. So a new drinking venue was sought in the familiar, fraught dockside bars. The streets behind were red light areas and appeared to operate like open-plan brothels. Within the rowdy Harbour Lights pub, a rhinestone-covered Elvis impersonator with a distinct Scottish twang was busy twirling his limbs around, to a chorus of heckling.

"*Aye*, can *ye* do requests? Get *tee* fuck then!"

They settled in at the Harbour Lights. At the bar, below lines of dimpled glasses hung on hooks, Tim bumped into two diving colleagues. While ordering from the offerings spelt out on a peg-letter board, Tim included two extra drinks in his shouted order for former workmates who wouldn't consider it a decent night out unless they were punching people. So to facilitate another "good night out" they told Tim, who had no reason to distrust colleagues who mentored his first steps in diving, to go and ask how much the pretty prostitute in the corner charged. He was in the process of dutifully doing so when her fiancé arrived back from the toilet, and was most unamused by the mistake. Then the punches, glasses, tables and bar stools flew. Tim's American co-workers lifted him out over their heads before both windmilling in on the poor innocent gent, who had merely been set upon for defending the honour of his intended. As Michael and Brian beat a swift exit from the flock-wallpapered fight club, the four became two pairs for the remainder of the evening. Not that Brian was too sad about leaving; he had never been fond of bars where pirate videos could just as easily fund a round of drinks as legal tender, nor where the patrons tended to hold their palms over a burning lighter as a show of fortitude, or indulge in bouts of arm wrestling. As they searched for a bar that wasn't likely to explode into another brawl, Michael joked he had had the rough end of the deal.

"Bloody hell. So I'm the one left going out drinking with the Burt Reynolds lookalike. I don't stand a bloody chance."

"Don't get your hopes up, Mike. Do you know how to tell the women from the men around here?"

"Tell me, matey?"

"The women's tattoos are spelt correctly."

They traced a nostalgic path through hazy bars either or both had frequented during previous work sojourns and it soon became clear that Michael's fears were unfounded. Most of the local ladies made it apparent that the English pair were as welcome as a turd in a Jacuzzi. To the ringing sound of the last order bell at 11pm, Brian and Michael headed back in the direction of their digs, only to stumble upon a discotheque within sight of their hotel. Despite Michael's insistence on dragging Brian inside Scandals, it was a fruitless end to their evening. The same could be said of Tim's night out. Blind drunk and mischievously avoiding arrest spraying two approaching officers with a water filled fire extinguisher, he was cornered next to a stairwell in a multi-storey car park.

"You're nicked, laddy!" The Canadian assailant was rapidly disarmed and detained.

"And you're wet!" was Tim's accurate comeback.

13. Good Ship *Galloper*

"It's a fishing boat?" Brian said, more to voice his own confusion than in expectation of an answer, as he was alone. "What the fuck is going on?"

The question to himself turned to steam rising past his nose. Ice crystals were beginning to form on the damp central portion of his moustache that brushed down over his top lip. He was clad for action of a different form; stood there in denim jeans, a thick blue fleece over a submariner's jersey and a battered bucket hat. Over his neck hung a duffle bag, straining to fit everything Brian needed to bring. In his left hand, he held his well-travelled briefcase. Brian still had the worries from his fleeting fit in reception on his shoulders, like an invisible yoke. It clearly placed in doubt his fitness to undertake what he had agreed to.

He asked for directions to the vessel by name, after walking the short distance from the hotel to the harbour. He followed them through the forest of masts and outriggers, thinking the advice was mistaken once he reached the ship, or, more accurately, trawler. Groggy and hungover, even after a morning shower, the aroma of cognac was still wafting up his nostrils from his moustache. Despite Michael's misgivings about attending Scandals discotheque with a film-star lookalike, Brian hadn't stood a chance either. The undeniable truth was that Brian had been the oldest patron in there and had felt it. Michael was not so far behind in those stakes, in a sweaty venue where the fashion was for the men to also wear eyeliner and fluorescent socks. How things had changed.

Peterhead, or "Peterheed" as the locals called it was dressed in white that morning, muted by a deep covering of snow. The surrounding roofs were so full of snowfall, that when the flurries stopped, the wind carried airborne powder avalanches down into the streets. Pavement kerbs and harbour tracks all hidden from view below the deadening, crunchy layer. The weather side of bare tree trunks wore a snowy film, pressed on by the overnight storm. Street lighting bathed Brian's slippery path to the docks in pale orange light. A slate-grey, snow-bearing sky raged past overhead. Brian watched the supplies more consistent with oil-field support being loaded onto the aft deck of *Galloper* by a creaking quayside crane. Brown helium and white oxygen canisters 50 feet long, each semi-containerised into 32 cylinder banks were being loaded in the hold, towards the bow to counterweight the bell and connecting living chamber due for loading on the stern. On the back of a waiting articulated lorry was an old dive system, yet to be lifted across as the driver sat patiently in his cosy cabin with the engine ticking over.

"Bit crisp this morning, matey," Michael said from behind Brian, his dander up after a morning shower. He wasn't displaying a shred of a hangover. Roy and Tim were yet to appear.

"Oh, you gave me a fright. Jesus, I feel a bit rough."

Michael lifted his gaze to where Brian's had been, watching the crane swing back and forth, "I wasn't expecting this."

"No, me neither. Are we meant to be diving or fishing?"

Moored in front of them both was a large fishing trawler some 200 feet in length. The living cabins and quarters were crammed together over the bow. Above this, a broad set of windows marked the ship's bridge. Two thirds of *Galloper* were ceded to a working aft deck spread 40 feet across, which was being cleared of snow by the small crew. The bull-nosed hull was coated pine green. The embossed cream lettering of the vessel's name painted on the bow was blighted by acne-like rust blisters. The arms of the wide A-frame crane were set back at the stern, over a rear deck that sloped off into the water and powered by a hydraulic ram either side as broad as the telegraph pole. Inside the bridge, with the wall heaters on full blast, the loading was commencing as planned, as observed through the binoculars of the dive superintendent and part-time medic, Gordon. Ex-Navy, tall, authoritative and a speaker of the Queen's English, the diving operations of *Galloper* couldn't be in more capable, fastidious hands. His standard work uniform was a collared shirt spilling over a sweater, straight slacks and glossed galoshes. The well-travelled Gordon had spent much of his working life in the Far East, based in Singapore – where poisonous sea snakes commonly basked on lower reaches of offshore rigs. He had begun as early as a baker that morning, coordinating the loading of the gas, the diving bell and double interconnected chambers of the system on which it sat, generators to run the water pumps for the divers' hot water suits and power air scrubbers to recycle helium from the divers' exhaled gas. The dive control room, full of dials, switches and screens was housed in a prefabricated hut, fixed up tight behind the main superstructure. The compensator mechanism had had to be retro-fitted to the A-frame, to balance out the effect of surface swell on a submerged diving bell; this was the concluding delivery of a bare-bones setup. The two supervisors Davide and Sergio were due to board later that morning.

By contrast, sharing the sauna-like bridge with Gordon was the not very commanding Captain Shenchenko. He was a seafaring Ukrainian bear of a man who was perpetually pouring nips of rum into his coffee from half bottles. His hairy back and undervest were clearly visible through the thread of his bleached collared shirt. Pattern baldness had removed all but a detached central tuft on his shiny crown. His Russian and Albanian crew were occupied on deck with preparations, relieved not to be hauling any nets on their next voyage, so spirits appeared upbeat. Their instructions were passed down the microphone of the ship's address system, Captain Shenchenko blinked on every word spoken with a voice from the back of his throat. Brian and Michael, after assessing that the job was being conducted somewhat on the cheap, stepped up the gangplank. These would be their last steps on terra firma; they bounced up the springy walkway, grasping the rails for help with the weight of their personal cargo.

With a blackened right eye and a tale to tell, Tim reported for duty next. Still in the same red hoodie and knuckles grazed through "*self-defence*", he claimed, in a second scrap of the night at a disco. His mentors, who had sparked the initial orgy of violence at the Harbour Lights, had exited the scene soon after with hardly a scratch on them. The same couldn't be said for the locals who had foolishly joined in the tear up. Rage and alcohol imbued pluck, were no match for years of combat training. The number of victims recovering by morning in local accident and emergency ward was proof of what can happen when drunk Scottish dockers engage with a pair of ex-special forces divers. With Tim in tow, the follow-up later in the evening had been a bruisingly successful skirmish with all three having to flee a nightclub, dodging vengeful knife gangs in the icy surrounding streets.

Roy had sat peacefully in a corner of the Harbour Lights, supping his pint of beer quietly as the fighting ensued and injuries mounted up. Collected and unruffled, he had even made a trade with a surviving local, once order was restored and the wounded had been treated. Rolled up like a Turkish carpet under Roy's left arm was a polar bear skin, its head and enormous curled claws protruding from either end. "What's that bloody thing?" Brian asked; he had been the first the see the fourth melodious member approaching from where he stood in the group.

"How do, boys. It's a polar bear skin. Bloody heavy I tell ya. Bought it off a bloke with one ear in the pub last night. He said it was the last one to be sold in Stavanger in 1970."

After two steaming cups of tea and a doorstop bacon sandwich each, Gordon treated his new troupe of intrepid divers to a tour around the ship that ended out on the rear deck where they inspected the layout of the diving system. Brian relished walking over the gritted steel sheets enclosing the hull; they had a satisfying bounce similar to the sprung dance floors in the nightclubs he had once managed. The specifics of the voyage and gold salvage had been imparted to them earlier on the bridge, when they were introduced to the skipper.

A 1,100 nautical mile cruise headed north-east out of Peterhead at eight knots would take six days to round the western shoulder of Norway. Perhaps a day longer to return if currents were inclement. The Barents was every bit as menacing as the North Sea, and three times the average working depth. The nearest port would be Honningsvag, south-east of their site by some 50 nautical miles, on the Norwegian tip of the border with Russia. During that voyage Michael, Tim, Roy and Brian were expected to assist in hooking up the compression chamber to the gases loaded in the hold of the deep-sea fisher, routing through the supervisors' panel in the dive control shack. From there, Davide and Sergio would monitor the gas composition and pressure of the divers' sealed living environment and diving bell to simulate the working pressure. The sole purpose of the main living chamber was to continuously store the divers in relative waterless comfort at the equivalent pressure to what they would encounter outside of the bell. With all trace of nitrogen removed from the habitat and their bodies saturated with a blend of helium and oxygen only. This allowed for decompression to be carried out only once on completion of the job, rather than after each dive - the controlled lowering of pressure equalising to that found at sea level.

Water supplies were required: salt water for the oversized wetsuits which pumps would heat before feeding it down a diver's umbilical, and fresh water for the living chamber. More frugality of planning was on display with the gas reclaim unit, which was also in need of a power supply. It was designed to reduce the amount, and therefore cost of gas required. Based on Gordon's calculations, they would set off with an oversupply of ten percent, if the reclaim scrubber remained operational and able to recycle elements of the spent gas. The arms of the aft A-frame were sufficient in length to lift the bell, off the deck-based chamber and feed it down to the wreck from over the stern, once the divers had transferred under pressure and were sealed inside. This action would repeat twice daily as the diving teams would swap every twelve hours.

Gordon fetched a polaroid camera from a cabinet draw in the dive shack and smiled as he asked the four aquanauts to hold their positions for posterity, "Brian, Roy, turn around for the camera and say cheese."

"Oh, OK. Tits and teeth, *Broin*. Tits and teeth!" Roy advised, as they shuffled into the frame of Gordon's viewfinder with the others.

The engine note rose and the ship shuddered as *Galloper* slipped her moorings, the ropes cast back onto the deck from the dockside. It was early afternoon but the sun was beginning to check out for another day, perhaps feeling it was wasting its time above such thick, low cloud. On even waters within the harbour, the town of Peterhead was a mosaic of white roofs. Through the gathering haze, gas refineries and storage facilities on surrounding treeless hillsides had their normal bleakness softened by the recent whiteout. The top of the balustrade enveloping the hull of *Galloper* supported a capping of powder snow. As a backdrop to the beginnings of such dirty work, the surroundings seemed almost pristine.

Of the two supervisors, only Davide had made it before they left. Sergio had been delayed clearing UK immigration from his flight into Heathrow airport from Brazil. He would join the ship in Norway from a supply vessel, once the divers were already in saturation, depending on how long the set-up took. Davide, who hailed from Lyon, had wavy parted silver hair on top of a triangular face, with full cheeks and narrow dark eyes. His collected, composed nature was well suited to his job, and his wit would sometimes make the divers job a pleasure. He had brought a small number of plastic frogs to place in the dive shack. Chosen from a much greater collection in his Aberdeen office; all gifts from colleagues and contacts alike, testament to his considerable *bonhomie*.

With the bow of *Galloper* cutting through the smooth waters within Peterhead docks like a tailors shears through a sheet of satin, the North Sea opened up before them. A bilge pump discharged unwanted ingress from the ship in an ever-drooping arc of water that cut a line parallel to the hull on the sheltered surface. Tim and Roy watched from the bow as the gap to the land widened. A trio of terns floated above them like sea-swallows, in a V-shape. Spray carried on winds by the bow that was beginning to thump through growing waves, lifted the hair on their necks. Roy was already in his greasy orange overalls and a set of red ear defenders were pulled back behind one ear to hear Tim if he spoke.

"That's more like it, old *Gal*," Roy said gladly. "I wonder what's down there, you know? Ships have been visiting this harbour since the Vikings." He went on to quietly mouth a sea shanty to himself, one sung by the crew of colliers when leaving ports along the southern coast of

England. It was a rhythmic clarion call for a fair and safe passage to their trading destination:

We'll be back to port soon, my Sally

Away to sea we must go

Open the sails, man the rudder

We are headed to Plymouth Hoe

Well, pour another rum, Jack

Let those currents be true,

Fill the sails with your best, and...

Bring us back to shore, Jack

14. Press down

The diving system had been fixed to the deck longitudinally, placed centrally within the footprint of *Galloper's* hull to minimize how much the movement of the ship would be felt within the pressurised chamber. The end onto which the bell would mate was positioned nearest the stern, within range of the A-frame lift. It was 50 feet in length and powder-coated in baby blue, like a flightless fuselage or beached submarine. The larger living area consisting of two thirds of the total was separated by cylindrical trunking from a smaller enclosure where the bell connected on top and the divers would transfer between both whilst under working pressure. This "wet room" also housed the toilet and shower, where ablutions were performed. Both sections were six feet in diameter and constructed with a gauge of steel thick enough to maintain pressure of 420psi, a comparable working depth the divers would be stored at throughout. It was similar in breadth to a small private jet. Inside, green vinyl bench bunks were affixed in pairs to the chamber walls with just enough space for a body in between. In the cramped, confined space, furthest from the trunking leading to the separate wet room compartment were icy metal benches around a stainless steel table. The scent was musty and metallic with just a hint of body odour leftover from its previous use. The sealed entrance, trunking and the airtight service hatch through which daily meals and drinks were transferred, were all circular. A lone porthole either side allowed for inspection by the supervisors or

Gordon, the superintendent. It also granted those trapped inside a fraction of natural light with a view of the deck surrounds. The floor was metal sheet plating in the living chamber, perforated grates for drainage in the wet room directly below the diving bell.

For transport to the bottom of the ocean, some 80 storeys down, the closed diving bell was a far sturdier beast. It was designed to tolerate external pressures 28 times greater than the one atmosphere measured on the deck, while retaining two divers at an internal pressure equal to the working depth. The walls were cast four inches thick and sealed shut with a round door, set centrally in the floor and locked with a vault-like wheel. Enclosing the teardrop shaped bell was a supportive, protective frame of pipework four inches in diameter. This structural exoskeleton, painted a contrasting tangerine, was formed of two horizontal rings with four curving vertical struts that each exceeded the height of the bell and ended with a convex capping. Onto which were fixed gas cylinders - an independent stock of heliox gas, in the event the topside supply should fail.

As their northerly latitude increased, the temperatures began to plummet. On the balmy bridge of *Galloper*, the outside temperature was reported at -15°C. Briny spray from the bow froze on contact with the deck. Icicles joined together down the balustrading into serpentine columns of opaque ice. With the use of heaters, four sweaty bodies and the conductive properties of heliox, the living chamber would easily sit at a clammy 28°C once fully pressurised, regardless of the weather outside. Under the choosy, watchful eye of Davide, the fishing crew were guided through their rudimentary tendering duties for the voyage, using whatever skills they already possessed that could be transferred. These included changing a gas line to the correct cylinder in the hull and in which order. When to apply or loosen the external brace around the trunking between the bell and chamber, and where on deck to coil or feed the bell umbilical as part of the procedure with deploying the divers. Most important of all, given that three of the four pressurised pirates were British, was an unceasing supply of pots of boiling water through the service hatch into the living chamber, for brewing cups of tea.

Communications checks were passed to and from the bell via the dive shack and the repeater speaker in the supervisor's cabin, which had been fitted at Davide's insistence. All the sensors within the split habitats analysing the gas mixture or temperature were functioning correctly on the supervisor's panel. So was the motorised winch wheel of the heave compensator that had since been added to the A-frame. When the stern rose, to atone, an equal measure of umbilical was released and retracted back in again when it dropped. The generators and pumps had all been run for sufficient time for the divers to be satisfied. The pressure tests on both sections of the chamber had been signed off; the last had been left overnight without any significant drop recorded, so it was time to enter their home for the next two weeks.

Until Sergio joined them on a supply vessel along with the last fresh supplies to be taken aboard, Gordon would fill in and supervise back to back with Davide so the divers could be pressed down – a dry, virtual journey down to the seabed. It would take three days to safely reach the simulated working depth of 915 feet in the chamber, at which they would remain until the decompression started. This was ample time for Brian to contemplate his cognitive dissonance in placing himself in this position. The chamber looked cramped, as all their effects were moved over a morning from the relative comfort of their dorm cabin to the inside of a metal tube. Tim and Roy, being the tallest, would have to stoop the most often. A number of meaty head-bangs were always going to be heard before their proprioception and instinctive movements attuned. Having drawn straws outside by the door that would soon enclose them all in together, Brian discovered his bunk next to the inlet vent was most undesirable. Trying to sleep next to constant rushing of heliox gas being injected to maintain pressure in the chamber would be a challenge.

Brian enjoyed and had missed the unbuttoned informality of being out at sea. His last clear view of the outside world was a spectacular, if very cold one. The sky thinned for the first time in days, revealing an endless set of rippled clouds, like seemingly infinite ribs of a fish skeleton. Not a finger of land or tiny island broke the misty horizon in any direction. If Brian did experience problems during his first press down since the decompression fiasco with Malcolm in Brazil, he couldn't be further from medical attention. He lit a final cigarette and offered another poking up from the packet to Tim, as they milled around like condemned men waiting to face a firing squad. Isolation from the boat, its crew and the marine world around them beckoned once again. A mermaid-like lure of gold at the bottom of the ocean had been their recruiting sergeant. They were heading for a contained world where only the blackest humour would sustain you and the two options for a relaxing stroll were either on the seabed, or around the wet room. Not an option for your average claustrophobe. And there would be a no-man's land of nine days of safe decompression between them and a return to the outside. Hair and nail growth would all but cease at this pressure. The vocal chords pitched higher and higher as the amount of helium increased to substitute nitrogen, which was toxic at such depths, from virtually the first breath. Taste buds went on strike to such an extent that food might as well have been fried cardboard, fed to the blindfolded.

The estimated two-week run around the clock meant Brian and the rest had 14 dives to complete. Twelve-hour bell runs in teams of two was nothing new for seasoned oilfield divers, nor for the supervisors, who would also swap with each changeover. While one team was working on the salvage from the bell below, within the living chamber the other would be sleeping, eating, perusing soft pornography, drinking tea, playing a Ludo-like board game adopted from the Royal Navy called Uckers or preparing for the next shift. Like the curved internal walls, the outer surface of the whole diving system was shiny wet. The surface temperature was above that of the surrounding frozen ship, so no ice formed on the exterior. Inside the living chamber, the moisture gathering on the walls would evaporate once the heat rose, creating humidity levels akin to downtown Jakarta.

Brian drew the last few pulls on his cigarette, dropped the butt between his boots and extinguished it with the tip of his sole. Privately pensive, he filled his lungs with fresh sea air, waiting for Tim to conclude, before offering a gracious, guiding palm towards the circular entrance.

"Magic. After you."

"Why, thank you. Hurry the fuck up now!"

Bell politics ensured they all had to get on. The omens were good if the time already spent in each other's company was a guide. Those who rocked the proverbial boat would rarely be given a chance to extend their diving careers with an invitation back. For the most part, egos had to be parked, feelings were bottled up and, most difficultly for Tim, tongues were frequently bitten - all for the greater good. Friction or grudges were as detrimental to safe operations as a dose of food poisoning would be to the quality of the air they breathed in the pot. No drinks, smoking soothing cigarettes or mind-altering drugs after a shift. And it was advisable to follow the normal unspoken rules in British pubs to ensure cordial discourse: avoiding the subjects of religion, politics and money.

Brian waited as Tim pulled himself through the circular opening. With rising unease, he stood alone for a few brief seconds. His lower jaw was pushed out in trepidation. Up his nostrils, he filled his chest with arctic air and exhaled slowly through round lips. It was an irrational, anxious feeling he had never experienced before on previous hitches. In addition, it was an instinct his doctor would encourage Brian to obey, given the pressure his body and brain would soon be under. He had completed many hundreds of dives without drama; a handful not without incident and weeks at a time spent in saturation before. He had 15 years of experience to draw upon to settle any nerves he felt, but most prominent in his mind's eye was his last deep outing. Standing a few steps from the open chamber, he remembered the fears Malcolm had experienced on his own return to saturation; they now felt visceral and familiar. The only witness to Brian's unease was Rolan, an Albanian crew member, moonlighting as a senior dive tender, having proved his aptitude to Gordon during the brief training. Rolan waited for Brian to give him a wink and climb inside before pulling the round door closed and spinning the wheel lock. With a brush and bucket, Rolan soaked around the seal with soapy water to check for signs of bubbling air leaks, before raising his thumb, an agreed signal for Davide to proceed in the dive shack.

Inside, they were shielded from the noise and whine of pumps and generators, which was replaced by droning vibrations from the same source. Michael was preparing his lucky draw of an upper bunk; the penthouse berth opposite was occupied by Roy, already stripped down to his underpants and tattoos. His thin mattress was covered with the polar bear skin, with its open-mouthed head down at his feet. Both the beast's right legs and savage array of claws were draped down over Tim's bunk on the lower floor. Either side of Tim's lap was a book and a Rubik's cube. His Walkman headphones were already around his neck. Almost immediately after Brian took in the scene, through both portholes they watched emerald green fishing nets being draped around the lower sections of the entire diving system, a crude attempt at cunning camouflage. The bell remained exposed above the chamber for operational reasons, rendering the whole idea futile should a spotter plane fly overhead.

Michael was the first to comment as the helium and oxygen mix began to rush in through the vent below

Brian's bunk, his voice an octave up already. "Mmm, interesting chaps. I wonder who we're being hidden from? Norwegians or the Ruskies? Looks like they're covering us up."

"Eh, it'll look like they've caught a blue bloody whale with a growth attached," Brian said flippantly.

"Well, I don't care as long as we find the gold, do you?" Roy replied, peering through the opposing porthole with knowing eyes, as the sea salt in his voice box was replaced with helium.

They all exchanged glances and nods in agreement with Roy. It wasn't their lookout to arrange the documentation to notify relevant governmental bodies of the salvage. They were being pressed down to retrieve whatever the relevant paperwork, which might or might not exist, pertained to. Bas would carry the can, should things go badly. They were just following orders!

Brian waited for Michael to neatly arrange his space and slide a lacquered black suitcase under the bottom bunk. From it, he removed research material he would pore over, about another wreck sunk near his Norfolk home. Brian tucked the long side of a threadbare blanket under Michael's mattress to form a curtain for his bed below, a veil that offered a modicum of privacy in such an intimate space. Behind it, he could face his dread alone by pretending to sleep. If he got a headache or partial paralysis, which was what Malcolm feared the return of most, Brian would have to come clean and the salvage would be down to just three divers.

Through a piercing loudspeaker above the U-shaped seating area, Davide's unruffled francophone tones were transmitted from the dive shack, "*Bonjour*. I will take you down nice and slow, boys. No rush. We should '*ave* you at working depth in *zere* when we reach *ze* site. Sergio will be joining us tomorrow, shame we '*aven't* met '*im* yet. Good luck to you all and let me know immediately if you '*ave* any problems. Sit back and enjoy *ze* ride, gentlemen." As his goodwill statement ended, the injection of gas and associated hissing increased, Brian closed his nose between his forefinger and thumb to clear the accumulating pressure in his sinuses.

"What the fuck are you doing, Brian?" he thought to himself. It was too late to change his mind.

15. Dive Number One

When they reached the correct pressure in the chamber above the wreck site, a further drawing of straws decided Brian and Roy would carry out dive number one of a possible 28. Before entering the chamber, pre-dive checks up in the bell had been exhaustive to assuage any doubts until the four divers were 100 percent confident in the set up. The umbilicals, gas valves, comms equipment, and hot water supply had been tested. The four emergency "bailout" cylinders, smaller than a normal scuba tank, to be carried on each of their backs, were at the correct mixture for the working depth, albeit an extra fraction richer in oxygen compared to what was fed into the helmets.

They would be the first pair to dive on the wreck, which was unfamiliar as yet. The airlock door to the living area was sealed behind them, as was the next one they passed through the narrow pipe trunking to the smaller wet room that connected the two habitats. Brian was reminded of the customary whine, jolts and jars transmitted through the bell lifting cable as it took the strain. He heard the trunking up to the bell from the wet room being vented to break the seal, so the bell would release off the system once the outer clamps were manually removed by the deck tenders. They were now working under the supervision of newly arrived Sergio, who had an unexpected North American accent, given that he had such a Hispanic sounding name.

Brian volunteered for the first dive during the twenty-minute commute in the bell, down into the darkness. The concave walls of the bell shone with condensation in the light cast by a bulb wired centrally into the ceiling. All Brian and Roy had was the spatial awareness of how the bell was dropping in relation to the ship above. The actual depth, visibility, currents and proximity to the wreck were yet to be felt for the first time. Information that Brian and Roy would feed to Michael and Tim while changing over.

Captain Shenchenko watched the closed bell drop through the screen of his sonar, which he normally used to locate fish stocks. With no perception of the world outside, Roy and Brian were perched opposite one another on fold-down seats, sandwiched between coils of umbilical with the bell door at their feet. Hot water suited and wellington booted, they heard the rumble of the rear thrusters maintaining *Galloper's* location fade out to near silence. There was just a faint growl of diesel generators transmitted through the bell's lifting cable. Brian had already pulled the O-ring down over his head; this was the black latex neck scarf that formed a tight seal and held it in place above his collar. On his left knee, bouncing nervously, was his helmet. The kidney-shaped bezel edging the glass faceplate was fixed in place by multiple screws through the chrome housing. The circular mirrored regulator that both fed and reclaimed gas through the exhaust port, resembled a miniature discus, protruding below the glass window. The flow valve to where the umbilical and bailout tank attached was mounted against the diver's right temple, both linked via a polished pipe that curved through 90 degrees between the two components. The lemon yellow fibreglass outer casing sat below a horn-like central handle, inserted above the glass bezel top and similarly glossed in finish. Across the rear rim of the helmet was a low profile weight spanning between both ears like a horseshoe. Next to Roy was the bellman's band-mask, a lighter alternative to fitting the normal diving hard hat that was generally a two-man operation, checking each other as they went. The front profile of the band-mask was identical to the regular working helmet. But from there backwards was an over-long neoprene cowl that extended out to sit on the diver's shoulders, beyond the neck opening of the suit.

A spider of 5 wide legs like notched rubber belts held the hood snug in place around the rear of the bellman's head by fastening to proud pins around the minimised face plate the hood also hooked over. One of the rubber spider's legs was left unattached to allow for fast fitment in the event the bellman was asked to rescue his diver.

In reference to Brian's moustache, Roy offered some advice to pass the tedium caused by three days of being caged. "I thought you would've taken that beauty off already. Won't you struggle to get a seal?"

"Yeah, it can be a bit of a *baastard* sometimes, but I'll give it a try," Brian replied, his voice just as high-pitched as Roy's.

Through a crackly speaker above their heads, Sergio's cigarette hardened voice boomed from the microphone of his headset.

"Ok, guys. We're nearly down on the bottom. The wreck should be to the right as you exit the staging. Who's taking the first shift?"

"*Broin's* going down first. I'll be bellman, then we'll swap," Roy replied towards the speaker while pressing the transmit button.

"Ok, bud. Start getting ready down there."

Something didn't seem kosher about this blowhard American-sounding supervisor with a Latin name. More Texas than Tijuana, Brian thought. He couldn't put his finger on it but he wouldn't be able to just pop into the dive shack to check, when dive number one was complete. Brian clipped the underside of his helmet to a webbing strap joined to his body harness, to combat the one effect that was impossible for the supervisors to recreate in the pressurised dive system or bell – buoyancy. Without the chinstrap, the gas inside his helmet would lift it up tight against his chin for a 6-hour shift.

A few jerks felt in the bell meant the brakes were being applied to the lifting winch, finally checking their descent. They watched for confirmation that pressure in the bell had equalised to that outside as the seal opened minutely until a faint pop could be heard. Until then, the door would have been nearly impossible to open. Roy turned the wheel lock on his hands and knees as Brian fixed his helmet into the neck scarf. In the weak light inside the bell, when the door was lifted up on its hinge, the water lapping up in the trunking was black as pitch. Before Roy pulled his fingers from the handle and started to uncoil Brian's lifeline, he addressed the water, "Hello darkness, my old friend! Ready for your lucky dip, *Broin*?"

At comparable depth back in Brazil, during daylight hours in good visibility, Brian had been able to make out the dive support vessel with the illuminated bell dangling underneath on what appeared to be a cotton thin thread. At the opposing end of his and the bell's umbilical stretching up to the surface was his life, wife-to-be, stepdaughter, friends, family and fortune. On the cusp of the Arctic Circle, a repeat of those diamond-clear conditions would be unlikely. Sergio informed Brian of his expected duties, once he dropped off the U-shaped grid staging under the bell door. "We got lights on the bell, bud. You should be fifteen feet off the bottom. Just have a circle search to start with, to find the son of a bitch. We might have to move the boat if we aren't close enough. Good luck and tell me when you're on the goddamn bottom."

"OK, topside. Just leaving the staging now," Brian replied through the microphone placed by his mouth. "Can you turn the lights on? It's darker down here than the stout my mother drinks."

"You got it, bud."

Sergio flicked the switch for the bell spotlights on the panel in the dive shack, illuminating the scene for Brian the moment his feet landed in the sugar sand. Without taking a step, he stood up to his waist in a haze of sediment, absorbed the scene and passed on his first impression.

"Fuck me!"

"Everything swell, bud?"

"It's a big *baastard*," Brian noted before his gaze had finished arcing aloft at a hull that stretched ever upwards.

The seabed was softly flat and moonlike, fading out into back scattered darkness. Cargo was strewn in the debris field: cases, oxidised metal structures, errant goods and armaments that had once been fitted to the deck formed dark shadows across the sea floor. Double the length of *Galloper*, the wreck was stood upright as if still sailing with her stern, which had been riven by the mine strike, sunk deep into the sand. The hull was upholstered with a biomass of sherbet pink sea fern, which the current stroked as it passed along the structure, lending more credence to the impression that the ship was still in motion. Over these there were thousands of brittle starfish with plate-like bodies and snaking legs. Ribbon-like eels darted for cover when Brian got too close, where the bow sat on the sand.

"The boat needs to move about 50 feet to your port side. There's a current running and more drag from this reclaim umbilical. The gas is very cold. Visibility good though."

Brian retired back to the safety of the staging while *Galloper*, with the bell suspended underneath edged closer into the wreck. His right glove was constantly flexing in a futile attempt to warm the extremity; his damaged index finger had begun aching the moment he had left the bell.

"Ok, Brian. Ship moved and fixed back in position. You can continue. You'll be looking for a section already blasted out of the upper starboard bow."

"Magic. We're much closer now. Can you up the flow in my suit, it's fucking freezing down here."

"Sure thing, bud."

Near the end of the range of his lifeline, Brian located the section blasted out by the first salvage operation. As there wasn't the usual belt of torpedo armour in the wall of the hull, Brian just threshed at the steel sheeting, which broke apart like soft slate. After a somewhat boring six-hours as bellman, sat on his seat reading a scruffy newspaper in his under-suit rolled down to the waist, Roy would go on to be the first to enter the wreck. But he immediately stirred up a fog of residue and silt that failed to settle enough for him to begin clearing a path. Brian watched his remarkable partner return to the bell like an amphibious marine creature. For all his awkwardness on land, once Roy hit water his movements became silky and deliberate. So much so that Brian became convinced his partner might have had a set of gills. Completely at ease in his preferred element, Roy entered the bell and began removing the harness that carried his bailout cylinder as Brian coiled his umbilical, preparing the bell to be lifted back up and locked onto the dive system.

"I couldn't see a shitting thing in there once I stirred it up. I even sat there still for a good 30 minutes."

As Roy's cylinder bounced on the rubber matting covering the floor, it nudged the bell door. Brian lunged with his foot to stop it falling, but only succeeded in using his left ankle as a doorstop – a 75-kilogram doorstop. Brian watched in slow motion as it came to sudden halt against his joint with a wince-inducing "thunk".

"FUCK!"

Roy lent over to lift the door off his partner's foot and showered Brian in seawater still running off his dry suit.

"You alright, mate? Think that might sting a bit, *Broin*." Brian was unable to answer, such was the pain and steady realisation he would be limping for weeks thereafter.

With patience and dexterity, Michael reached the secondary bulkhead where the remaining bullion was thought to reside, during dive number two. Having cleared some ordinance and timbers out of his path, he placed them in the cage that a crane would lift at the end of the dive.

"It's darker than a coalmine at midnight in here!"

Tim followed up to take a title of his own – the first to enter the "gold room", 20 feet in from the outer skin of the ship. This was only to discover it was home to a rather territorial monkfish who didn't take kindly to guests. Without a single movement from himself, the space suddenly clouded with silt in his torchlight, stirred by the occupant as it prepared for an ambush. The first Tim knew of this problematic barrier was a flash of its flat white belly past his face and the lower jaw of the huge mouth clamped around the helmet. A row of teeth like numerous bent nails of ivory scraped the pane of his helmet as its tail, equal in measure to one of Tim's legs, writhed and twisted, trying to tear a chunk from his person. Extremely startled and with his head in the mouth of a creature similar to himself in stature, Tim fought the violent jerks and turns his host was inflicting on his neck and began to crudely head butt the bulkhead with the crown of his helmet until the thrashing stopped and it had sprung a dribbling leak.

Davide, who had swapped with Sergio for dive number two, heard Tim's cries and subsequent thumps through his headphones.

"Tim, *iz* you ok?"

"Fuck man. I just had a monkfish biting my head."

"I'm sure you dealt *wiz zit*?"

"It sure bit off more diver than it could chew. Ugly fucking thing. Biggest one I've seen."

"*Zhey* taste good, no? Maybe you should bring it up and I'll get *ze* chef to bake *ze* thermidor, no?"

Tim might as well have been blind trying to locate anything in the gold room. The 40 years' worth of sludge, residue, marine growth and monkfish shit had been whisked up into a pea soup. Once the leaking helmet was factored into Davide's culinary suggestion, Tim grabbed the tail of his flat-faced foe and retreated from the wreck. The determined climb up his umbilical carrying the 50-kilo catch, made him draw hard on his gas line. Once he reached the relative safety of the staging, he recovered from his efforts while aligning the fish below the trunking into the bell. Michael was stood over it, dutifully winding in his partner's umbilical.

"1, 2..." On 3, Tim pushed the fish up through the trunking, spiny head and teeth first. Once he heard his partner's screams abate, he followed on up behind. While the bell was locked back onto the dive system for the next changeover, Brian and Roy waited beside the area directly below the bell door. Twelve hours' worth of stale, rusty water would shower down when it opened before Tim and Michael exited. But there was a delay. Roy and Brian exchanged quizzical looks before Brian took one step forward for a clear view up into the bell. This was the moment Tim chose to launch the fish down through the trunking with a most persuasive stomp. Brian was already kitted up in his hot water suit and twisted his torso to glance the falling beast off his right shoulder.

"Fuck me, Tim!" Again, Tim waited for Brian's displeasure below to quieten before poking his head out over the aperture, pulling a devilish grin that plumped his stubbly cheeks up like cushions.

"Bloody right," having just shoulder-checked the catch, Brian affirmed in support of Tim's subsequent plan to pass on their Monkfish through the service airlock. But with the added sprinkle of wicked surprise, by concealing it in the soiled bath towels that were removed daily.

16. Bar Hatch

"Howdy y'all. What's happening on our dive together today, bud?" Sergio asked of his divers as he took the chair and headset Davide had kept warm for the past twelve hours.

"Right, topside. *Broin* is just leaving. His gas supply is open," Roy confirmed to Sergio while watching his partner step down the narrow trunking, back into the bitter water. Brian had increasing doubts about the identity of the mysterious supervisor they had never got to meet. Brazilians weren't often given to say "Howdy" and two years living in Rio gave him enough knowledge to know that neither did they use "Y'all". The more he heard of Sergio, the more Brian's chin stuck out and eyes squinted in unverifiable suspicion that he was being supervised by Charles Raynor again – the man who had nearly killed both Brian and Malcolm through incalculable, wilful incompetence. A walking, talking widow-maker on legs. But what were the chances?

Apart from the bell to topside chatter, all he heard in his helmet was his own breathing. Rhythmic and controlled, he pushed and pulled through the regulator, its valves creating a rushing tone distinct in their opposing flow. Each deep breath was loud; every expelled exhalation of gas not being reclaimed boiled under his chin before bubbling over his glass faceplate. Once orientated on the staging with the overhanging cliff face of the hull just discernible, wearing builder's gloves and gumboots he swam towards the aperture he would be entering through as Roy fed out Brian's lifeline. With a dive each from both teams, the agreed approach from their pooled knowledge was to avoid stirring up the target area inside the ship too much. Tim had found it troublesome to adhere to this method when he had found himself in the jaws of a monkfish.

So, on limping into the wreck for his first look on a swollen ankle, Brian pared his movements to the minimum, taking slow, deliberate steps with minimal fanning of his hands to correct his balance. The umbilical connecting at various points to his right side was run high around his shoulder to minimise the chance of it snagging around or needlessly brushing against objects covered in residue. The general movement out of the gold room, and latterly the wreck, would wash out more growth and sediment with it than could regenerate or be deposited between changeovers. Tim had hopefully ridden the gold room of its solitary tenant on his first access.

Brian confirmed his penetration into the wreck to topside, his struggle in doing so was evident to Sergio from the frequency and demand of gas interrupting Brian's speech. "Right, I'm in. Floor feels sound. I took my time. I reckon I've got algae rooting on my bailout. But..."

"But what, buddy?"

"I still can't see shit." He peered into the khaki cloud his minimal movements had caused. "I can hear and feel something banging though. Comes and goes."

"We think it's a section of loose plating towards the stern, buddy. The current must be catching it. Michael reported the same during his last dive."

"It sounds like someone hammering."

"So the room you're now in is 20 feet square, buddy."

"I'll take your word for that," Brian confirmed as he snapped one of four glow-sticks before letting them drop to the floor that was strewn with jetsam; through which he would begin four hours of aquatic braille. To his left, the corner closest to his entry point was clear, so Brian slowly moved timbers, shelving racks, glass bottles, jeep tyres and pipework of various gauges to that locale. Brian knew from his and others' salvage successes in the past that gold of this quantity would be underneath everything else in that room. If a single bar had been tossed into the sea, over time it would settle against the bedrock, beneath any surface shingle. And it would still shine as bright as the day it arrived on the seabed, no matter how long it had spent there. The only growth it could succumb to was a rare blue coral, given the right conditions.

The longer the bars remained undiscovered, the more the tension of failure grew in the air. The prospect of a successful salvage had never been a racing certainty. For all the planning, intrigue and allure, let alone the personal risks Brian was taking to be part of this operation, another band of hyperbaric bandits could have been along in the two years since the first salvage. The success of the initial job had ensured the location of the site was open knowledge, give or take a square kilometre or two. A competing recovery operation could have just sailed over the horizon with the bullion the day before *Galloper* arrived. Until one of the divers working unseen below, had at least one bar in his hand, only the "no pay" side of the arrangement was assured. Apart from his own route, Brian saw no evidence down there of recent disturbance in the gold room, so hope remained.

An hour of laboured clearing swiftly turned into two. The effort levels in shifting the tangled matter were beginning to tire Brian. He took breathers by telling Sergio he was waiting for the visibility to clear. On the few occasions this approach actually worked, Brian saw mirrored pockets of spent gas had formed against the steel ceiling like clouds of mercury. Working blind without the aid of pictures beamed back to the dive shack by a remotely operated vehicle (R.O.V.), Sergio gave the same information to Brian that Davide had tried to guide Michael and Tim with.

"If it helps you, they should be in wooden crate boxes bound with copper wire – ten to a box. But we don't know if the previous company even reached them, buddy."

"I reckon they didn't. It's a huge mess in here. Bloody shit everywhere. I can see why they left some behind."

The debris was stacked at its highest in the back left corner from the entry point in the room. Brian's clearing and shifting of materials built up in the near left corner that was clear on his arrival, most of the room was now accessible for a proper search. Rather than move all the random objects stacked in the far left corner, Brian began pushing his arms through gaps in the matrix to feel for the bulkhead, or wooden crates wound in copper cord stacked against it. He worked clockwise towards the entry/exit point at six o'clock during his final scheduled hour before switching to bellman for Roy. Brian's hands had groped a great majority of the contents of the gold room. He had a hardening conviction that the remaining gold had been salvaged already.

He pulled a horizontal section of timber from an accumulation in the far right corner, to make room to thrust his arm through. The heavy weight suggested a long substantial timber. While turning and pulling the length free from the mass, he felt the load drop dramatically following a dense thud closer to his feet. Brian immediately lunged his more dexterous right arm downwards into the opening towards the sound; his fingertips brushing straight across the top of the smooth, weighty object. He forced his shoulder harder into the gap, an extra inch or two for his fingers to reach around to the underside. Once his fingertips had the merest purchase, he lifted the unknown article out through the opening made for his limb and held it in front of his helmet for a conclusive view.

It was a trapezoidal form, ten inches in length, just a shade under four inches wide, a good two inches thick by Brian's estimation and about eleven kilos on the scales. A single bar of gold. Gleaming as much as the day it was cast and minted in Cyrillic script, it was brilliantly flawless in finish and worth a fortune. The ingots raised off the *Dalhousie* and traded with Swiss Christian looked homemade compared to these industrial-sized cousins.

"Yes, you *baastard*!"

"What's happening, bud. You found some commie gold down there?"

"I got one. From the far right corner."

"Yeehaaa! Good on 'ya, buddy. The cage is down on the seabed already, so go drop it in and we'll pull it up."

Brian had no energy to prolong a search during his remaining bottom time, after having found this momentous prize. A mist of sediment poured out over both shoulders as Brian reached the outer hole and dropped down to the seabed past the bell. His short descent quickened under the extra gilded load. A brief looping search brought him to the lip of the basket cage, where he leant his torso over with the slack lifting cable pinned to the cage by his left hand. As if laying a baby down for the night in its cradle, Brian placed the booty in the base of the cage and bid it a safe passage to the surface with an approving pat.

"Righto, you can take the cage up now. I'm heading to the bell."

"Roger, buddy."

Roy was even more excited on hearing of the find; his affection for all sunken treasure found him celebrating in a peculiarly British fashion. He leapt to his feet, waved his fists triumphantly in the air and bent down to his ankles with the removal of his under-suit and underpants. In a flash, he stepped into his wellington boots while fitting his bailout and harness. Next, the band-mask helmet went on swiftly and was hooked up to his bailout as he moved over the exit and down he went. Without the benefit of prior warning, Brian was just beginning to climb up his umbilical, having positioned himself so it fed perpendicular to the bell above. He made the error of looking upwards to check his path to find the most unsavoury sight of his streaking bellman sliding down the same umbilical with one or another arm pumping above his head, as if sliding down a firemen's pole.

Brian shook his head demonstrably and pointed an index finger upwards. Roy had rejoiced enough and was verging on becoming hypothermic so was extra swift in his return to the bell. Brian wisely waited a minute or two as Roy made himself decent and felt his lifeline resume being run around hooks to coil it again.

"Fucking hell, Roy," Brian commented, after receiving help to remove his helmet, his face full of a grin, despite his physical exhaustion.

"Sorry *Broin*. I got a bit excited there when I heard you'd found the first one. I had to celebrate a bit. It's good for morale, I've found," Roy dryly replied, shuddering as he got back in his under-suit and without a shred of shame in his smiling eyes.

"Christ. I've seen some things down here, but that's a first. You must be bloody freezing?"

"*Broin*, I can't deny I'm not warm. Last time I did that, I was in the tropics," Roy shivered.

Roy was soon reheated by the warm water supply in his diving suit as he took over the search from Brian. He went straight back to the corner where Brian had hit the jackpot 30 minutes earlier. Over the span of Roy's shift, three more bars were added into the lifting cage. Each was smeared in faint veins of oil fuel that was scraped off up on deck. For all the unseen jubilation and celebrations between Brian and Roy 900 feet below, once the gold showed up on *Galloper*'s rear deck, the mood among the topside crew shifted to palpable paranoia. It was a floating island of people out for their own gain, and now there were terrific amounts involved. Green-lit by greed, one particular team member's desire to up his stake was ignited as the crew fussed over the success of the initial find, Brian would eventually realise.

17. Bubble Trouble

A weather front whipped up the waters of the Barents, beyond the safe capabilities of the heave compensator. So they waited. Without the security of having recovered four bullion fingers, the time ceded to poor conditions and dives aborted would normally generate anxious frustration in the chamber. Instead, it was a jovial bubble of satisfaction on an otherwise fraught ship. Genuine fears of boarding by Russian coast guard or navy was shredding the nerves of Captain Shenchenko and his crew, leading to the gold being hidden in secret compartments throughout *Galloper's* hull. They needn't have been so worried. Without current newspapers or English-speaking pirate radio stations, they weren't to know that Russia's latest leader had passed away (the third in three years) the day the bell first visited the wreck. A political vacuum endured for five days until the promotion of Mikhail Gorbachev to General Secretary of the Soviet Communist Party.

The pots of hot water for making tea were passed through the service airlock with great frequency, all with an accompanying waft of a burning hashish reefer. The deck tender charged with emptying or filling the airlock under the trust of Rolan, who perpetually had an extraordinarily plumb "*cigarette*" drooping from his lips. The crew were known to congregate around the chamber during periods of downtime between duties, amazed at how the divers stored within could tolerate living in such restrained peril. Bas had been updated via his mobile phone, apparently while he was in a towel at his local sauna club; his elation was tempered by the news of lost dive time, further reducing the window available to the operation. Bas would make a huge loss on the proceeds of only four bars, as it stood.

"Has it crossed anyone else's mind we should keep a few of these for ourselves? I mean, nobody can see what we're doing and we're told there's thirty-two in total. How could that ponce Bas know they didn't take more during the original job?" Tim suggested at one point.

Michael was first to respond, "I don't think we should go down that route, matey. I'll be happy if they pay my expenses to be able to do this salvage."

"Are you crazy?"

Brian interjected to diffuse the discussion. He didn't have to be an economist to see the benefits. "I think Tim may have a point, you know. It's a bloody magic idea if you ask me. We're taking all the risks, don't forget."

"I don't mind, boys. Whatever you decide, I'm good with," Roy added, increasing the votes for to three, to Michael's one against.

"A little dicky bird told me they tried to take a bar each on the first job, but couldn't work out how to get the *baastards* up without being found out."

"So we'd have the same problem, wouldn't we?" Michael asked while emptying another cup of tea.

"Well, in theory, yes," Brian confirmed before elaborating on Tim's scheme. "But where there's a will, there's a way.

Looking at the bell frame when I was down there, I could see a bar fitting inside the uprights; couldn't you? One in the bottom of each, behind that domed end cap?"

The length of the ensuing silence indicated that Brian's idea appeared sound. As it did to Sergio, who just moments before had arrived in the supervisors dive shack to tell the divers to get themselves ready while slipping on his headphones, Sergio picked up the chatter on the open channel from the chamber, after delaying pressing the transmit button for just long enough.

The weather had improved, which they could also sense in the chamber, crammed around the lipped stainless steel table behind their bunks. Through the speaker, Sergio's informed voice blared, "Start kitting up guys. We'll stick to the same working teams so Brian and Roy will carry on with me from the last dive. We've only lost two of a possible 28 dives. And if you are planning what I just heard you talking about, then I want in too, buddy!"

Brian mouthed a silent "shit" to his colleagues. He unfolded an old newspaper flat, picked up a biro that had been rolling around the table with the motion of *Galloper* and wrote the following across the clear footer below the inky text. Once everyone had read the message, Brian screwed it up into a tight ball and threw it inside the bin – his suggested means of disposing of any future notes:

IF WE ARE GOING TO DO THIS – WRITTEN NOTES ONLY

Roy could see that Brian looked a little below par and offered to take the first stint. Brian didn't argue. After only two dives, and a week held under pressure in total, he was feeling the pace. He always equated working at great depth to working in a custard that thickened with the effort of each dive. Two years out had left him ill prepared for the rigours of a vocation that had never drained him so much before. Roy appeared sprightly in comparison, and looked keen to return to the dark hypoxic water, his natural element. Twenty-eight bars remained to be found as Roy made a gurgling, bubbling exit from the bell.

"Slack the diver, Brian," Sergio requested as Brian watched the staging below empty as Roy pushed off towards the wreck. "More slack, more slack."

"Roy's very quiet down there?" Brian said through the intercom.

"Just keep slacking him until I say so, buddy."

"Is his mic broken? Why can't I hear him in here?"

Brian's misgivings towards Sergio and the few seconds of unsettling silence from Roy brought about a visual search around the bell for where his equipment was placed. Holding Roy's umbilical in his left hand, Brian shuffled around the trunking exit to bring the transmit button within easier reach.

"What the fuck is going on? His mic was working before he left. Now he's not responding?"

"Listen, buddy. You goddamn divers aint paid to think, you asshole. Do what you're fucking told, buddy. Slack the fucking diver!" Sergio ranted. Unannounced to his team of divers below and in complete dereliction of duty, he had momentarily shut off the gas supply to the bell from his dive panel. In complete affront to his rank of responsibility in the operation. Brian as bellman was unaffected during the short outage in his pressurised sphere. Roy was not so fortunate.

Sergio knew he was on borrowed time with his new identity and every commission thereafter may be his last, so he had to make each opportunity pay. Later, Brian would reflect that this was the first evidence of anything remotely Latin about Sergio, other than the name. His fiery nature was in fact more consistent with Brian's experience of Brazilian norms, or perhaps a Texan who had lived there too long and married too frequently.

"I don't need to think as I know what you're doing. What else could've happened? We tested everything. I'm going to get Roy." With that, Brian stopped giving slack to his diver and supervisor. As bellman, he preferred to be semi-kitted up, rather than Roy's more relaxed approach of rolled-down under-suit, some Old Spice and a crossword puzzle. With his index finger on the simplex transmit button, Sergio kept ranting through the speaker, unable to hear replies from his bellman. While Brian pulled the band-mask over his face, time began to slow down. As he opened the valve on his bailout tank and connected it as a single feed, he passed a rope through an emergency hoist before clipping that through a ring fixing next to the caged bulb fitting in the ceiling.

"DON'T GO OUT THERE, BRIAN! IF ROY'S TOAST, THAT'S HIS PROBLEM, PERIOD! AND MORE LOOT FOR US! WE CANNOT RISK LOSING ANOTHER DIVER. DO YOU FUCKING READ ME?"

If Sergio hadn't been blocking the bell to dive shack communication, he would have heard Brian say, "Bollocks to ya. I'm going out on my bailout, so I'm safe, you *baastard*." He had been in the same situation himself in Brazil and couldn't just stand there and let things be, sitting helpless and unwilling.

Brian exhausted the bell, raising the working depth by a couple of feet, which partially flooded it up to his waist. He had no comms nor particularly wanted any, no hot water supply and only about four minutes supply of gas. He squeezed down onto the staging, fading out Sergio. The immediate jarring cold took all the air from his lungs. This was his first taste of exiting the bell without his hot water supply flowing. Roy's motionless umbilical was dropping straight down, which was not a good sign. Wedged between the bell and staging exit, Brian's hands grabbed opposing sides of his partner's lifeline and heaved upwards in a tug of war with an inanimate opponent. Levering with his legs, each lift brought Roy back closer to rescue. Pulling across the staging, he reached further to replace his grip each time as he stood up, only to fall backwards onto his tailbone, using his body weight as extra leverage. The fifth motion lifted Roy, whose limp body was twitching, to within arms' reach of the staging. Brian secured one hand under Roy's scarf, then reached around with the other before prising his partner back onto the staging. Brian's bailout supply was increasingly hard to draw on and his range of muscle movement were restricted in the breath-taking cold, so he knew his time was nearly up too. One rope end was lashed, tied and knotted around Roy's harness across his chest.

Each pull of the line through the bell hoist raised and then held Roy, allowing Brian to guide him aloft through the tight trunking if his protruding kit or umbilical snagged on the way up. Brian's limbs ached with cold for the final few tugs, his bodyweight a more reliable source of counterweight in raising his partner's head clear out of the water and making sure his boots were not obstructing the bell door. Like a swimmer springing off the wall of a pool, Brian launched himself upwards through the trunking. Roy hung from the sternum of his harness, the weight of his helmet and head combining to extend his arcing neck over his back. As swiftly as his numb hands would allow, Brian removed his band-mask and reached for the lever to sufficiently vent the bell, to increase the pressure in order to lower the water level. Roy would have to be attended to in his position; some upright chest massage delivered through Brian's knee would be required. The bellman, who was now able to breathe freely, unclipped Roy's helmet before returning his head to upright to remove it. Inside, Roy's eyes were down, closed, and without even a flicker.

Not seeing a trace of life, once Brian had relieved him of his helmet, he braced Roy's torso with a tight grip on each shoulder before his knee was driven upwards towards his heart in compressions a second apart. On the fifth, Roy's neck stiffened and his eyes opened as if awaking from a deep night's sleep. Thankfully, for the patient and the responder, the kiss of life was not necessary. He looked around the bell and then at Brian shivering below him, with a deeply distressed expression, and spoke, "You alright, *Broin*?"

Brian was stunned. "You looked dead a minute ago!"

"What d'mean? Why am I hanging up here?" a confused Roy asked, while only his toes could touch the floor.

"I had to rescue you. Sergio shut your supply off I think."

"No? Why would he do that?"

"For your share? I don't know. All I know is you're alive, no fucking thanks to Sergio."

Yet to regain his full senses and scale of what just happened, Roy was more concerned with the condition of his partner. "You look awful. Could you let me down, *Broin*? I'm fine. I don't remember a thing." Roy's body had been saturated with helium and oxygen gas for over a week, so his brain was well supplied, and he appeared unaffected by his brief period of unconsciousness. When Sergio cut the gas source, Roy had remained conscious after exiting the bell for only a few moments, sustained by the dregs of gas left in the length of his umbilical. Once that was depleted, Roy passed out immediately, without a chance to switch to his bailout, midway between the bell and seabed.

Sergio had been silent during the rescue, but when Brian transmitted a message asking for the bell to be returned to the surface, he heard Davide and Sergio engaged in a curse-laden dispute. A few minutes followed before the lifting sensation started as Brian finally released Roy from the hoist and untied the chaotic yet effective jumble of rope.

"What sort of knot do you call that?" Roy joked.

"One that worked. If you can't tie a knot, tie a lot!"

"You are a wag, *Broin*."

Roy and Brian had set off for the seabed in good spirits, with little or no valid motive to indulge Tim's suggestion, other than for the hell of it. Now dive number four was returning to the surface, with no gold and Brian on his haunches until his strength returned enough to let Roy down from where he was swinging, with a cast iron basis to diverge from Bas's salvage plans. A fatality had not been priced into the deal, so the divers would have to secretly up their subsea demands. Brian was convinced that, if Davide had been supervising them, Roy would not have needed to be rescued. It was an unnecessary reminder for both of how quickly things could go wrong. Just seconds were needed for divers like Roy to perish and Brian's own personal roulette wheel would be spinning right up until he left the pressurised chamber to climb onto the deck.

18. Revolt

"*Turrrn ze fooking* gas supply back on now, you *bastarrrrrd!*" Davide ordered his colleague upon breaking the frozen seal on the dive shack door, his trill R's rolling as much as the ship. "What *arrre* you doing?"

Davide had sprinted from his cabin in such a rush that he was only partially dressed. Knowing diving operations had recommenced with Sergio at the helm, Davide had just eaten and was in the process of realigning his sleep pattern in his cabin for the later shift. Dive number five was due to begin at noon, four hours later than usual. Davide was therefore due to swap with Sergio twelve hours later at midnight. He had just removed his winter jacket, loosened his paisley tie and was slipping off his shoes on the bed edge, when he heard Brian and Sergio's exchange through the repeater speaker. With only a single shoe removed, Davide's bothered brow drooped with concern as his attention switched to interpreting the frantic events unfolding 900 feet beneath their ship. He sat there for a few brief seconds, mulling what to do, until Sergio's shouting started. In a single sweeping motion aimed for the door, Davide pulled his sweater back on, swung the jacket onto his right forearm before attaching his left through the opposing sleeve and trod down the heel of the one shoe just slipped off. Such was his haste, he nearly tripped over the watertight door lip exiting out onto the aft deck. He opened the dive shack entrance on Sergio, whose index finger was jabbing towards the diving panel, in full rage. Sergio's face was purple with anger, his parted silver white hair and Van Dyke style beard further highlighting the violet skin tone. But he had just been caught red-handed, deploring Brian to not even attempt to rescue Roy.

Davide stepped into the dive shack, stamped his foot into the hastily fitted shoe and lifted a shirt collar clear of the neck of his diamond cut sweater. He couldn't believe what he was witnessing, Davide's head shook as his brain failed to summon appropriate words to describe the heinous act Sergio was committing. *Meurtre* would have sufficed. Unabated beneath a flickering strip light, Sergio kept screaming hot spittled abuse into his mouthpiece, oblivious to his impending demotion and cabin-arrest by Captain Shenchenko. Brian had already exited the bell to recover Roy when Davide pulled the headband of the headset from Sergio's heated crown. There followed a profanity-loaded tirade, a fulsome French take on British cursing, absorbed during many years spent in Aberdeen, as he removed Sergio.

"You *fooking wankerrr*. Get *yourrr fooking arrrse* out of *ze chairrr*. *You'rrre fooking* sacked. *Arrre* you *fooking crrrazy*? Get out of *zis* shack, go to *yourrr fooking* cabin and don't even *zink* about leaving it."

Sergio's inscrutable expression on learning his personal gold rush had been monitored was consistent with having part of his anatomy trapped in the jaws of a vice. He leapt from his seat to confront Davide, who was shorter by six inches. Sergio viewed square on was hip slim, but when he spun ninety degrees either way upon his axis, a sizeable lateral beer belly came into view, only restrained by a belt with an enormous buckle that pulled deep into his paunch like a button-back couch.

"Who are you to do this, buddy?"

"I'm *yourrr* fellow *superrrvisorrr*. But once Gordon knows you just *trrried* to *murrrderrr* one of *ze diverrrs*, you won't be anymore. So *fook* off *beforrre* I get *ze* crew to *rrremove* you."

Davide, not in the least bit intimidated by his puffed-up peer, counted to three inside his head. Then he dropped Sergio with a flashing left hook, in support of his previous notice of sacking. Robbed of any menace, as he lay groaning on the floor, Davide stepped over Sergio contemptuously and squeaked into the vinyl chair in front of the dive panel.

Since his arrival up the rope ladder from the Norwegian supply ship in two-tone shoes, Sergio had proved a truculent presence. His long-held view was that divers were just bodies in the operation, disposable elements willing to risk the most and easiest to bump off in a matter of seconds, if a financial gain or a contract renewal were the bitter harvest.

Eventually, the full story would come out. Since the bell had dropped on the ship in Rio and his subsequent discharge, Charles Raynor's professional reputation had been rightly tarnished. Unlike Brian's, the injuries suffered by the divers in Rio were of a physical nature, irrefutable in the face of a lawsuit. Spurred on by another disastrous marriage to a Brazilian bride and the crippling cost of her fondness for cocaine, he obtained illicit Brazilian identity papers from his Commando Vermelho contact. The same gangster he'd sourced similarly forged documents from, stating a younger birthdate on Brian's work visa in Brazil. So Charles Raynor had become Sergio Souza and, as Malcolm had predicted, put himself about in the job market to be picked up by an ignorant salvage financier whose only concern was the title "Diving Supervisor" on his C.V. and a willingness to work for nothing, should the gold not be found. Posing as Sergio, he hadn't even bothered to affect a South American accent; his Texan tones booming through the intercom had been making the bell vibrate for twelve hours a day.

The name aside, Brian should have spotted the familiar bravado and bullshit. Sergio knew exactly who Brian was and had purposely delayed his arrival on *Galloper* so as not to cross paths with his former charge. He had even peered briefly through the dive system porthole to lay eyes on the diver whose legal action he now viewed as the beginning of his own downfall with Marsat in Brazil. His identity would correctly prove a barrier for any savvy employer willing to conduct even minimum auditing of his references. Sergio had planned to delay the decompression long enough on the return voyage that he could be toasting his share with a Pina Colada a long way away by the time the chamber door opened. Brian had nearly died twice under his supervision. His latest victim, Roy, was still drip-drying in the bell as Brian blew exasperated air through flapping lips before getting back to his feet. Since he had left the bell, the icy waters of the Barents had crept deeper into his bones until it felt the marrow was forming ice crystals. His muscles continued cramping as his hypothermic body sought to warm itself from the shock. The intercom had been silent for the first half of the bell's recovery to the surface, until Davide's voice provided an update, sounding notably more ruffled than his customary cool.

"*Zat ass'ole* Sergio won't be supervising anymore. *Ze* Captain will '*ave* '*im* confined to a cabin. I just spoke *wiz* Gordon. '*E* will stand in for Sergio and supervise until we finish *ze* job."

After lowering Roy, who had been most patient, through the bell hoist and back onto his boots, Brian patted him on the shoulder and winked before satisfying his curiosity. He pressed his palm on the transmit button and asked, "Does Sergio have white hair, a white goatee beard and half rim glasses. Like brow-line, I think?"

Davide confirmed, dryly and with some satisfaction. "He does '*ave* white '*air*, '*is* goatee beard is now pink *wiz* some blood and I broke *ze* glasses when I first, '*ow* you say, chinned '*im*."

"Magic! Is he fat and wearing terrible aftershave? And talks a load of bollocks?"

"Yes, *zat's ze* one."

"I'll bet you my fee his real name is Charles Raynor. He's got a history of doing this."

"*Zat*'s a tempting wager. '*Ow* do you know *zis*, *Bri-yon*? I don't know *ze* name Raynor."

"Because he did the same to me in Brazil. And my partner. I didn't know for sure. But I do know, whoever it is, Charles or Sergio, they just tried to top Roy."

"I know what happened. I '*eard* it too."

"And that should have been me, we swapped on this dive."

"'*Ow* is Roy?"

Brian looked at his partner gingerly removing his harness and grinned as Roy lifted his eyebrows back at him, "I think he'll make it."

Until Davide reported the incident to Gordon and proposed the workaround to complete the salvage, he knew the divers would rather mutiny than trust their lives to Sergio. Gordon held the whip hand where the diving operation was concerned, just as Captain Shenchenko ruled his ship. Installed as Chief Justice, Gordon nodded in agreement to Davide's points and suggestions; his head shook like a forlorn, ticking metronome as he learned of Sergio's actions. There was no other alternative. They would be losing Gordon's eyes on the ship's bridge, but the grip which Captain Shenchenko held on the crew of his vessel was reassuringly tight. Sergio, lacking the moral fibre of recusing himself, was to be restrained in his cabin by the skipper, before being handed over to the authorities in Peterhead, without wider questioning into the nature of the voyage. Sergio submitted to the sentence once he got off the cold floor of the dive shack and Davide arrived back to see the ruling was carried out. If Sergio had thought his silence over the divers' furtive plan to increase their percentage would guarantee his share of the plot, he had read the room, or chamber, wrong. If you attempt to kill one of your fellow conspirators, you are breaking several clauses in any unspoken contract.

Davide had asked Michael and Tim to suit up earlier than planned. They had overheard some of the dive shack fracas through a speaker in the living chamber. Without Roy and Brian's side of the story and the ensuing radio silence, they were more perturbed than normal sensing the upcoming changeover, with the bell containing their colleagues nearing the chamber on the jarring A-frame.

Davide spoke cryptically over the chamber intercom: "On *be'alfs* of Gordon and myself, I wanted you to know Sergio will not be supervising you anymore. Gordon will be standing in for '*im* until we complete. Roy and *Bri-yon* can tell you why when you see them in a minute."

Davide had lost one diver during his supervising career, ten years earlier in the North Sea. And he had attended funerals of colleagues over the course of his diving life too many times to number. The images he held in his memory of the victim still haunted him, though it had been no fault of his own. The thought of wilfully taking a life was mindboggling to him. The sight of his diver, with all eight pints of blood drawn into a single swollen forearm like a balloon, having been sucked into a branch off a pipeline, was something Davide never wished to repeat. He had sent the diver down to inspect what had snagged the pipeline inspection robot; the culprit was the branch. It had only been held in place by the tremendous pressure differential created by the empty pipeline, laid on a seabed 90 metres below the dive vessel. With the slightest of pushes, the seal around the weld-line of the branch had been broken, and the diver's arm had been dragged into the opening, plugging until he lost consciousness and died.

Among the many silver linings for Brian of Sergio's removal, he felt could at least approach his principal, lingering fear of decompression with a percentage or two less apprehension. Davide and Gordon would see them all complete the salvage safely to the point of decompression – not a given after the evidence of Sergio's transactional style of supervising. More badinage and less big balls would follow.

Nonplussed and uncomfortable at being the centre of attention, Roy surmised his willingness to continue to his colleagues in familiar wry fashion; "I'm fine. I don't remember a thing!" His chest was sore from the thumping by Brian's knee, but his eyes were clear, and his voice was its usual gravelly growl, if higher pitched from breathing heliox. So no objections were raised to Roy escorting Brian on their next jetsam jaunt in twelve hours' time. They swapped with Tim and Michael to begin dive number six. When he heard the missing details of the truncated number five dive, it incensed Tim to the point that his neck flushed cherry crimson as he climbed up the stair rungs into the bell. But for their state of compression, Tim would very much have liked to pay Sergio a visit in his cabin. Michael hadn't overheard all the transmissions during Roy's rescue, but when factoring in his experienced ear, he could easily glean between the lines. This removed any wavering thoughts for such a normally straight arrow. He left a short scribbled note on a torn scrap of ruled paper in the chamber, which brought them all into accord. He tore off a few more for note exchanges inside the bell.

COUNT ME IN THEN – MICHAEL

19. Dive Number Six

After pinching up the knees of his trousers before taking his seat, Gordon dutifully took over supervising. He was unexpectedly wedged in behind the dive panel, deciding it was best to allow Davide to unwind from all the drama earlier that morning. Captain Shenchenko would be able to observe enough of the daily operations, and this, combined with knowledge of his own vessel, would make him a decent pair of overseeing eyes from his bridge.

Dive number six was far more fruitful than the previous, ill-fated attempt, a welcome boon in light of the time lost and last aborted dive. Working in the same clockwise direction, the systematic shifting of materials out of or into the clearest corner of the gold room was beginning to pay dividends. The uncharted areas in which the remaining booty had to hide were forever shrinking. Michael brought out five more bars during his six hours. Tim tenaciously found another three, bringing the salvage total to twelve, and was sure he had palpated two wired-wrapped cases matching the description given during the briefing. Each find increased the value of their negotiated share. Only 20 were now lingering in the wreck, if the estimates were indeed accurate.

Tim and Michael couldn't have wanted for a better stand-in for Davide, who had supervised their opening shifts. If there was something they needed, Gordon knew it the moment they did, if not before. If they wanted more time for the room to clear or a change to the flow into their hot-water suits, it was done without hesitation or question. All the communication from Gordon was insightful and Valium-calm. As the bars were loaded into and lifted up in the basket, more smuggling space in the hull was opened on the orders of Captain Shenchenko, in a flurry of commands growled through his bridge microphone.

The gastronome in Davide brought about a lengthy negotiation with the galley chef, as he insisted that the food served to the diving operations staff should also be served through the airlock into the chamber, rather than the vaguely seasoned "*cuisine*" normally slopped onto metal trays and dished to the crew as fuel in three daily sittings. The arrival of a pan of beetroot Borscht soup through the service airlock by the pot-smoking tender led to it being returned intact with many complaints. The fruits of this culinary intervention saw Brian and Roy enjoying Steak Diane for their main meal, followed by Pavlova for dessert. An ex-diver himself, Davide thought it better the divers were happy when living and working with such constant peril. The flavours wouldn't register either up the nostril or when passing over their palates, but the sight alone was a nourishing feast for the eye. Davide believed you do your best when at work, but you make an extra effort at dinnertime.

Brian hadn't been alone in misgivings about Sergio. He had rubbed most people up the wrong way with his brash opportunism even before he nearly murdered Roy. Gordon and Davide had already shared an aversion to their cocksure, supercilious colleague. He had seemed to them like the kind of supervisor who was only interested in the potential payday at the end. He clearly knew all too well how easy it was to cover up a fatality or act of incompetence, in a profession that had few equals for the associated danger. Sadly, they had gained too much experience of this attitude before. No professional care or duty had been on show when Davide burst into the dive shack to bring Sergio's supervision to a bloody and abrupt finale. During the changeover between dives six and seven, Tim gave further details of the boxes' location. By the time Michael and Tim shed their suits and were drying themselves in the dive system, they could absorb the silent words of another of Brian's notes.

CHECK OUT THE FRAME END CAPS ON YOUR NEXT DIVE?

Sitting opposite Roy, Brian's manner didn't reveal any of the unease he was feeling on the next shift. The aborted dive had stirred intense memories of being fed bad gas in Brazil. Apart from a slight sallow hue to his expression, Roy was just the same as he had been at the start of dive number five. Well-fed and refreshed from the theatre of twelve hours before, Davide was back behind the panel, his leather jacket squeaking with every movement in his seat.

"Roy, are you sure you're OK down z*ere*?" Davide asked of his divers. "Perhaps *Bri-yon* should go first again?" They both held a stare and nodded tacit agreement as the bell they were sealed in dropped down to *The Perseverance*.

From inside his recently fitted helmet, Brian spoke to topside, "OK, testing comms?"

"'*Ear* you loud and clear up '*ere*."

"OK, leaving bell now. Please ask Roy to keep slacking me. Swimming straight across to the wreck," Brian deliberately spoke in short sentences, each divided by a loud respiratory movement of gas.

In the area six feet short of the near right corner that Tim had pinpointed, Brian soon found the two boxes. Both were wound in oxidized turquoise copper banding; a single box was too heavy for Brian to shift more than a few inches over the debris-covered floor. In the beam of his torch, sediment rose from the lid like slow-motion smoke as Brian attempted to move it. He ran a set of pliers across the top, shearing each band until they were all cut. A flat screwdriver prized the lid open, further secured by tacks through the sodden sides, and a beige mist of wood fibres engulfed Brian. The void around the bars had been filled with deadening sawdust, which Brian emptied into the gold room with repeated waves of his hand over the surface.

Once cleared of the remaining particles, he reached through to sight the contents with his hands. He immediately realised that what he now saw posed a dilemma for their plot-within-a-plot; the 20 bars that theoretically remained represented an end to the salvage. And they were all there in front of him – side by side in boxes. Each was two feet long and dovetailed from corner to corner, 12 inches high and 18 broad.

"Are *ze* boxes open yet, *Bri-yon*?"

"I got one open. I'm in a cloud at the moment."

Starting at one side, Brian raked his fingers through the remaining sawdust, and across ten equally spaced ridges.

In his torchlight, he saw the flash of gold he had expected. But he wasn't going to let topside know that, just yet.

"It's empty. I'll open the other *baastard*."

"*Merde!*"

In the four hours left of his shift, Brian could have had twenty bars out and into the lifting basket before Roy was due to take over. However, the ability to secrete four of the bars in the frame structure surrounding the bell had still not been tested. Under the cover of allowing the conditions to clear in the gold room, Brian left the wreck to turn his attention to the outer frame of the bell. The rounded end caps were not fixed by an obvious weld around the adjoining circumference of the tubing. He guessed that the multiple layers of varying company paints further secured the capping in position after being pressed into place during manufacture. Although the prising open of the second box had revealed the final ten bars, Brian's reports differed somewhat from the truth again, to buy some time.

"The second one is empty too. Bollocks."

"OK, you '*ave* two hours left now. Please keep working towards *ze* near right corner," Davide advised positively, concealing his disappointment as his shoulders slumped. He knew from a record of the room he had sketched, including the areas that had been reported clear by the divers, that little of that space remained unsearched. "*Zhey* are probably still in *zere* somewhere. *Zhey* must be in *zat* right corner *zen*."

Three hundred metres beneath Davide in the dive shack, Brian's salesman smile within his helmet was so bright, he almost didn't need his torch. His celebrations at the find were mute for Davide's benefit. The number of bars was correct, even with four bars missing; everyone else involved in the salvage would still do handsomely from their respective arrangements. Twenty-eight bars recovered on a job expecting a total of 32 would represent an acceptable return for all. All the remaining bottom time could be divided between periodically recovering single bars, reported to have been found loose in the "unexplored area" and preparing the bell frame to absorb four bars without raising undue suspicion.

The point of the bell frame that sat furthest over on the chamber when mated on the system was the best obscured on deck. Brian spent his last two hours scraping the side-point of his screwdriver that had opened the boxes, through the thick coating of paint to scratch a channel clear between the frame tubing and capping. He improvised with one bar due to be recovered in the basket and used it as a weighty hammer, trying the shift the domed metal cuff with his screwdriver, transmitting the downward welts like a blacksmiths punch.

"Take your time, Roy. Both boxes are to your right as you enter the room. You can't miss 'em. I told Davide they're empty to buy us some breathing space," Brian whispered during their changeover. Roy nodded his agreement to Brian's plan to stagger the salvage of the remaining gold. "I haven't managed to get the end cap loose yet, it's the one when you head left off the stage."

"Righto, *Broin*," Roy confirmed as Brian handed him his helmet. "Was that you banging?"

"Yep!"

"Righto, I'll take a look. See you in six hours then."

Brian unhooked Roy's umbilical and fed the reels out through the floor as the new bellman watched his diver pat away a graceful, giant Grouper fish that had settled in the gap between the bell and mesh staging. Roy's inner pirate played his role perfectly during the quarter of a day he would be spending out of the bell. Brian felt his partner working on freeing the capping, before darting into the wreck to claim to recover a further ingot and recording the find with mock rejoicing on the intercom, to Davide's congratulations. An hour before they were due to be lifted up, Roy appeared unannounced up through the bell trunking and braced himself up on the points of his elbows.

Not wanting to speak through his helmet microphone for fear of allowing another supervisor in on their plan, Roy swivelled the end capping around in his gloved hands. A finger from his opposite hand pointed to two holes further up the sleeving normally seated inside the frame tubing. Through either hole, a soft rivet unseen by Brian had married the two sections together. A short-lived moment of triumph ended with Roy withdrawing down the trunking, after collecting an errant piece of steel wire on the bell floor. Brian gave his partner an appreciative thumbs-up as water began to pass over the mirrored pane of his partner's submerged helmet, the bubbles rumbled and spat as they burst. Roy pushed the end capping back into position and turned it until all the rivet holes were allied enough for the wire to retain it, before making another sortie towards the wreck like a kid sprinting toward a candy store. In character, he only brought out a solitary bar to add to the five waiting in the crane basket. Brian's earlier brace was doubled by Roy, raising the total reported recovered to 18 of 32.

"Magic. I didn't see those *baastard* rivets," Brian said as his hand slapped on Roy's shoulder.

"I just knocked 'em through, *Broin*. No problem," Roy replied, rubbing his eyes after pulling his face through his neck scarf. "I don't want to worry anyone, but I kept seeing a Beluga Whale while I was out there. I've read the ol' Ruskies have trained them since the sixties to patrol harbours or search for mines. And the one I saw had a collar on it. Quite friendly though."

"You serious?"

"Yeah, it came quite close. It's all white so pretty easy to see out there."

"Bollocks. That's all we need. In that case, we better get a bloody move on."

20. Bar #28

READY TO GO BOYS – END CAP READY – GET LAST 10 IN BASKET – 4 INTO FRAME

Michael and Tim dutifully replaced their colleagues in the bell after twelve hours of much needed sleep and scant recuperation, interrupted only by the serving of Davide's tongue in cheek catering order – a prawn cocktail with a round of de-crusted smoked salmon and cucumber sandwiches. Wearing a black roll neck jumper under his glossy parted hair, smoothed down by a recent shower, Gordon was handed the moist headset to speak to his divers at the start of another turn at supervising. Once the headphones were cupped over his ears, he adjusted the mouthpiece so it was at a comfortable distance from his lips before clearing his throat to speak.

"Greetings gents. Here we go again for another evening together. All looks good on the panel here. Any issues with you two in the bell there?"

"Nothing here, matey. Roy and Brian have left us a nice tidy bell," Michael said, failing to share the contents of the note Brian had wedged behind some pipework.

"Same pattern as yesterday? Tim to go first again?"

Tim gave an unhurried, exaggerated nod across to his bellman, who duly converted it and passed on verbally to

Gordon, as they felt the bell cut through the choppy surface of the Barents Sea. "Yep, Tim's going out first, matey."

"Great. You'll feel the bell come to a stop in a few minutes. Let me know when Tim is all kitted up and ready to go out there."

"OK Gordon, will do."

"The forecast isn't too bad for the dive today. But we're expecting some weather fronts to blow through in a few days, so it'd be great if we can wrap up before then, guys and head for home."

"Yes, wouldn't it. Let's hope so, matey!"

"I'll keep my eyes on the dials up here. Good luck gents," Gordon signed off, before opening the dive logbook, for a better understanding of what had been achieved during Davide's previous dive with Brian and Roy.

With stoic, eager effectiveness, Tim toiled over the course of his stint. He was largely blind in the familiar sediment cloud while gracefully floating down to the seabed through the entry point into the wreck, in search of the lifting basket. A stronger current on that dive meant the basket had come to rest further away than usual. The underwater winds had eased it down the starboard side of the wreck, which Tim could just reach at the full extent of his umbilical. Combined with much cursing aimed at the basket and himself, Tim tenaciously lugged the mesh cube to within working range, traversing debris over which he frequently tripped or slid, until he was within sight of the bell lights. Having originally unearthed the boxes on his previous outing, Tim knew exactly where in the room to aim for and viewed the exposed contents with wide eyes. The saturated sawdust, so long a companion in the sunken boxes with the gold, dropped away slowly from the smooth bars as they were lifted clear of their containers. Tim wiped each and brushed them clean of finer silt and sticky oil fuel while exiting the wreck. By the time he dropped it into the basket, every character of the cast Russian lettering was gleaming in his torchlight.

"I got one. Dropping to seafloor to place in lift."

"Excellent stuff, Tim. That's nineteen in total. Keep going down there. Let's see if we can make it twenty, sir," Gordon encouraged.

Such was his enjoyment at the comparatively speedy increase in the number of salvaged bars, Tim's scheduled six hours passed swiftly, despite the physical demands. Enter wreck (try to avoid being attacked by a monkfish) – recover another bar of treasure – float gracefully out of the wreck down to the seabed – place treasure in lifting basket – and repeat. Before Tim knew it, he was back safe in the bell, feeding out Michael's working length of lifeline. He shook the water from his thick mop of hair, which was soaked from the trickling leak into his helmet

What could have been the last dive on the wreck, one which very much had an end of term feel to it, didn't last very long after the divers switched around. They knew how close they were to finishing up and heading back to shore. It was like shooting fish in a barrel, Tim had recovered nine bars before Michael's turn to leave the bell. The solitary bar, making a record breaking ten to be sent up to topside from a single dive, represented Sergio's proposed share of the deal he had muscled his divers into accepting. That last bar, Michael's first of his shift, reminded him how weighty the metal was. It was impossibly heavy, making lead appear a lightweight cousin. Had Sergio not shut off Roy's gas supply, they would have been secreting five bars into the frame, instead of four.

Just when things appeared to be progressing smoothly, some painful reminders of potentially fatal outcomes in their chosen profession were lurking just around the next corner. Such threats could and would strike mercilessly, without a shred of warning. As soon as Michael's first bar hit the bottom of the basket with a dull clunk, his umbilical suddenly lifted and stiffened behind him. Simultaneously, Gordon slowly delivered some agonising news for the divers' plans.

"Michael, get back to the bell, please. Just a precaution. The Captain just reported the ship's positioning system is malfunctioning. Is the bell moving?"

"I can't see it from where I am, matey. But I can feel my umbilical's just got tight."

"Roger."

"You better lift the basket now then. There's about 100 grand's worth of gold in there now – you don't want that acting as an anchor, matey."

"Roger. No we don't. Lifting basket now. Get back to the bell, Michael. Tim, start pulling in the diver's line, please. Quick as you can, now," Gordon advised, almost sounding hurried. "I'll let you know if the system cuts back in up here. Let me know when you're back in the bell with Tim!"

Brian and Roy could hear the ship's rumbling thrusters cutting out to silence in the chamber, only the generators and pumps screaming on deck remained after that. If Michael had not jumped upwards to begin climbing his umbilical, he would have been dragged across the seabed and into or through God knows what lay down there. If the ship moved rapidly, the bell would sway behind like a pendulum. Despite the weight of the diving bell, basic physics remained the king. The more the ship above moved, the greater effect of the swing upwards on whatever was suspended underneath it, until the ship came to the halt and the bell would drop back to perpendicular depth. If the upward swing were too great or Michael's clamber up his umbilical were too laboured, he could get the bend he had always managed to avoid.

Outside the safety and constant pressure within the bell, Michael could ascend in terms of depth at a rate far in excess of the charts that safely governed the decompression process. Tim was also aware of this possible outcome as he pulled in Michael. Full of adrenaline and displaying the strength of a bear, he stood over the door and passed the lengths of umbilical over his shoulder. Suspended from the stern and helpless, Tim could feel the bell was no longer level as the list grew. The compensator fitted to the creaking A-frame was unable to correct all of the erratic drift of the ship across the squally surf. This translated into having to save his partner while experiencing effects in the bell comparable to severe air turbulence. The capsule jumped up and down like a lure on the end of an angler's twitching rod. Tim got no reply from Michael as to his condition and position, apart from an occasional grunt or curse.

Michael just kept focused on the next point his hands would move up to on his lifeline, as he pulled upwards as much as he did forwards, like shimmying up a rope, albeit one that had already swung to 30 degrees off the normal vertical – the more the ship moved, the more that angle would increase. When the movement of the drift of the ship and the malfunctioning compensator combined, it took all Michael's strength to pause his climb and just hang on while he was tossed and spun around as his umbilical cracked like a whip. The ebony-black icy water rushed past his body as the lights on the bell slowly became brighter. Half his umbilical lay strewn up around Tim's feet as he continued to draw his partner closer. His penultimate lunge brought Michael onto the staging, whose hands had seized up with the effort of the strength-sapping climb. One more pull from Tim got his partner up into the bell. Michael's inelegant entrance traded form for haste to clear his feet of the door. It needed to be sealed to maintain the divers in their pod of constant pressure. Michael gave Tim a laboured thumbs-up to close the door and seal them in. A moving bell wasn't a rare occurrence; early attempts at positioning systems in the North Sea had required transponders be placed on the sea floor for the system to communicate with and accordingly adjust. But these were prone to interference, ironically from divers' bubbles among other things. So drifting diving vessels were almost commonplace. Both Michael and Tim had experienced similar before and thus knew that the safest course of action was to get both divers sealed into the bell until the wandering ship was back under some form of control.

"No problem, man. I got your six, brother!" Tim cried as he leant over Michael to detach his partner's umbilical mountings.

Gordon provided an update on the situation over the speaker, "Were going to bring the bell up. The ship still seems to be on the move. If we lose you both off the end, we obviously don't have a spare bell to send down for you to wet transfer into."

"Bell is sealed now, topside. Take it away," Tim transmitted in reply.

"Right, bell lifting up now."

"Fuck. OK."

"Excellent work, gents. You've taken the total up to 28 bars."

"Just four of them left in there, eh?" Tim replied, perfectly aware each of those had a divers' name on them.

"Well, let's hope our skipper can get the ship back in working order, shall we? Because, if we need to return to shore, we'll lose too much time on this job. So fingers crossed we don't have to leave those last four down there."

"Roger that," Tim added then turned his head to Michael and pulled his lips down to one side in an inaudible pained gesture, before plainly mouthing the word "fuck" to his partner, with his hand clear of the bell's transmit button.

"See you soon, chaps," Gordon said.

Apart from Sergio's attempted murder of Roy and some conditions that had not been favourable for deploying the divers, the operation had gone smoothly. They had not expected a technical issue to render their plans of subdividing the loot inoperable. It wasn't as if they could just slip on a pair of swimming trunks, jump over the side of *Galloper*, and recover the last bars while holding their breath. Owing to unforeseen circumstance, something almost to be expected in their industry, their attempts at skulduggery may have worked against them. The deficit in their percentage from salvaging less than the expected target would be easily surpassed by a hefty section of Russian gold reserves each. But if they were unable to return to the wreck, the decision to recover "their" bars last, while maintaining the pretence of a search ongoing, would prove a foolhardy one. All chances of another dive on the wreck now rested on the sweaty shoulders of Captain Shenchenko up on his sub-tropical bridge with a yellowed cold war computer running the positioning software, stored on a floppy disk. He was currently beating that computer with a disapproving palm of his hand as the alarms on his bridge continued to blare.

21. Framework

"I 'ave good news and bad news. And more bad news for you guys!" Davide advised, spinning a crowned plastic frog around in his fingers in the dive shack like a set of worry beads. The bars on the electric floor heater that warmed his legs were glowing amber like molten magma behind the chromed cage surround. Brian and Roy were due to fulfil the next and what increasingly looked like the final dive possible on the wreck.

Pensively, Brian pressed the transmit button in the bell, just after locking themselves in and their colleagues out. "Right. Good news first I guess?"

"So, *ze* ship's positioning system is working again."

"Magic. That is good news," Brian agreed, although he had known that already, having heard the thrusters restart and reverberate.

"It's been running as a test for *ze* last four 'ours, so we called you both into *ze* bell. We are back to where we were now."

"And now I'll have the bad news."

"The bad news is it might stop working again. *Zat's* not *magique* is it?"

"No it's not!" Brian admitted as he pushed his jaw forward and squinted at Roy, pondering what the follow-up batch of misfortune would be. "And what's the second bit of bad news then, Dave?"

"*Ze weazer* front '*eading* our way is turning into a big *bastarrrd*. It makes no sense to sit it out '*ere* in *zat* if we cannot dive for a week."

"Oh, right, Dave it doesn't. That's a bit of a *baastard*."

Roy and Brian both looked upwards at the moisture covered bell speaker as Davide gave his assessment. "So my suggestion is *zis*. If you find *ze* four bars in quick time, brilliant. If *ze* system plays up again, return to *ze* bell and I'll bring you up and we'll '*ead* '*ome*. If *ze weazer* changes as we expect, again, I will bring you guys up and we'll call it *ze* day, yes?"

Roy shrugged his narrow shoulders and nodded in hushed understanding of the suggested dive plan. Brian scratched at the short stubble on his mandible, "OK, sounds good to us. Let's go for it then. We need to get a move on."

"Agreed, gentlemen. We '*ave* 28 bars already. *Zat's* 89 percent of *ze* total. So not bad, we'll all do well out of *zis* job regardless."

No more written notes between teams were needed, they all knew where the remaining gold was, what they had to do to recover it and by when. This was probably their last dive and therefore, their last chance. Wearing only tattoos and rolled down under-suit, Roy would remain on semi-naked standby as bellman while Brian carried out their planned plunder. Roy connected the hot water feed to Brian's suit. The comms cable, gas and bailout supply were fixed into their respective housings to the right rear of his helmet. Moments before Brian sat the helmet over his head with Roy's help, he made a final request to his boisterous bell partner.

"Once we're done, please don't come out and bloody streak me again, for fuck's sake!"

By then poised to begin slacking his diver, Roy's sparkling eyes opened wide with amusement. "I can't guarantee that, *Broin*! I get excited!"

Conditions were poor, as was the visibility when Brian leapt off the under-bell staging. The opaque water was milky, like morning mist and running along the channel between the bell and the wreck at a tremendous rate. It was a clear augury of the weather system of which Davide had forewarned during their casual pre-dive briefing. He swam wide of the entrance of the wreck, to the up-current side of the hole and allowed the force of the flow drift him to his target. Inside the wreck, he was sheltered and unhindered. With all four bars stacked and cradled up in his arms, he realised the prospect of making it out and across to the bell frame with nearly a hundred weight in gold bars was too ambitious. They could be moved more easily in pairs, in two trips. Which was less than ideal given Davide could order Brian back to the bell at any second, were Captain Shenchenko to lose control of the positioning system for a second time.

While claiming to be sifting through the uncharted area in the gold room to topside, Brian left the wreck with a bar of gold pushed down into the sides of each of his wellington boots. The extra weight pulled him down swiftly as he jumped out of the wreck, back into the current. His only way to reach the bell was by pulling himself across on his umbilical. He wriggled around to wedge himself in the gap between the frame upright and the capsule it protected, hooking his legs around before pushing himself downwards until the back of his knees were supported on the bottom horizontal ring of the frame. Below his lap was the prepared end cap, held in place only by wire. Brian pushed his index finger through the rounded loop which Roy had formed so the wire was secure and began to work it straight to release it. His intermittent grunts or curses, all audible to Davide, lead Brian to improvise with the truth in response.

"*Everyzing* OK down *zere*?"

"Yep, just got my arm caught reaching through some timbers," Brian lied, while actually clinging to the side of the bell. He followed it with another untruth, trying to give the impression he was working at an appropriate tempo. "Room is nearly clear, not much left to search now."

"Excellent. Keep going down *zere*."

When the wire was straightened enough to be withdrawn, Brian cupped the end cap and removed it with partial downward twists. His need for a third arm suddenly came to the fore. How do you support one bar inside the frame with one hand, while cupping the end cap in the other, then gather the second bar from your other boot too? After a moment's deep contemplation, Brian achieved this by winding the wire tightly around his wrist before the first bar was inserted in the tube of the frame. Then he swung the knee of the leg transporting the second bar against the open end of the tube, thus bracing the first and bringing the second within reach. In a single, swift motion, the second bar was in his hand. Keeping the first in place with his knee, Brian stretched for the end cap, precariously tucked against his chest in his bailout harness, and pushed both bars up into the frame with it as he secured it temporarily with the wire poked through a single side.

Two up, two to go!

After a brief visual check of how the end cap was holding under the load, Brian headed back into the wreck, which Davide believed he hadn't left. Within minutes and in another cloud of sodden sawdust and other matter, his boots were re-lined with gold and the wreck was finally just that – a wreck. No treasure remained according to the records, reducing it to another sunken relic. Just one of millions of similar wrecks, slowly decomposing: sunken evidence of a maritime blunder, scuttled in the archives and nearly 300 metres from the closest view. That is unless you were the fearless few with the specialist expertise to survive in a sausage-shaped chamber, then climb into a diving bell. Descend down to the least explored reaches of the planet to access a shipwreck breathing a pressurised blend of helium and ever reducing oxygen in doing so.

Along with Tim, Michael and Roy, Brian was one of those willing, daring breed. For audible effect, he shifted some materials around as he stood over the bare boxes and emitted sounds of exasperation, before making his final, heavy-legged exit. Like Tarzan about to swing across to the next tree, he stood on the inner cusp of the wreck with only his toes breaking the passing current. He pulled his umbilical tight up to the bell. When ready, he sprang up and kept climbing arm over arm as best he could. His umbilical beneath him danced around in the current like an angry serpent, as the slack hanging off their attachments generated more drag.

Brian climbed onto the bell frame and shimmied himself back into the position from where he had loaded the first two bars. He thought it prudent to release the end cap under support from his hand and covering knee, in readiness for adding the third and fourth bars as he had with the second. Both his knee and hand strained while taking the weight of two bars, before he pushed the third into the frame. Then he repeated the trick. But the increase from three to four bars almost saw both limbs fail as he fought to re-fit an end cap under the weight of 90 pounds of gold. The void through the tubing the improvised retaining wire had fed was now blocked, so Brian poked the wire through both holes externally, running it around the profile of the frame that would be least visible from the deck. He rubbed his hand over anything looking even slightly like grease, something oil based or just dirt, before transferring the accumulation around the join, to age any fresh edges of chipped paint and fill any obvious gaps.

The salvage job was at an end. With the maritime misdeeds complete, Brian announced in mock disappointment that the room was clear and nothing else remained, hoping it didn't sound too much like a celebration in Davide's ears. "I'm back where I started. The room's clear. We've combed the whole area. The floor's still sound in this last section so we shouldn't have lost anything into the space below. The current's ridiculous and the visibility's terrible. Even worse when you shine a torch into it. Do we call it a day, Dave?"

"Roger, *Bri-yon*, head back to *ze* bell. Well done for your efforts today."

"You're most welcome. Just leaving the wreck now," Brian claimed while actually loitering just off the staging, out of Roy's view.

"Four divers and we're four bars short. Coincidence? OK, between you and me, whatever you are up to down *zere*…," Davide paused to make Brian sweat. He froze, waiting for Davide to continue. It soon became apparent that the divers' attempts at subterfuge and bluff hadn't fooled one supervisor at all. And they needn't have been so secretive as David was a highly astute man. "I '*ope* it's worth your while. You jolly deserve it I say – a lot more *zan* us sat up '*ere* on our fat arses. I'm sure Bas won't be too '*appy*, but *fook* that *arrrse'ole*! We got 90 percent, *zat's* enough. If Bas finds out about *zis*, it won't be because of me. Once again, well done and my most sincere *zanks*. A pleasure working *wiz* you all," He said all this with a certain paternal pride.

Brian neither agreed nor disagreed. He simply replied, "Diver heading back to bell," bringing the subject to a permanent, amicable close, he hoped. He was not quite in the clear yet by any means. Yes, their plan had seemed to work out well to that point. But the part of the job Malcolm had warned him about most, and that he had found so troubling himself, was the long decompression as a finale.

When Malcolm had first gone back into decompression, the memory of his and Brian's experience had flooded back as soon as the whistle of the escaping gases started. It had been bad enough for Malcolm to never want to repeat the process again; he had stuck to supervising ever since. Nine days of decompression beckoned, the virtual dry-ride back from near 30 atmospheres of pressure down to one, out on the deck. The creeping memories of the onset of paralysis had haunted Malcolm, and this was also a constant, rational fear of Brian's, in light of the experience that had so nearly killed him. It had taken two years of convalescence thereafter to recover some of his former self. He thought of Doc King's last words to him. Brian would be just as vulnerable decompressing inside the chamber as the concealed gold was, out on deck. In light of the depth of the salvage, nine days of terrified tedium was all that stood between him and a wealthy life back on land. Or it all could amount to a memorable send off at a lavish, money-no-object funeral service, full of stunned relatives, none the wiser about Brian's reasons for choosing this adventure and ending up swimming with the fishes under the Barents Sea.

22. Decompression

"You alright, Brian? You're looking a bit pale, matey," Michael asked from his bunk, having lifted his gaze from reading a ship's records. Michael had seen healthier faces on a pirate flag.

"Yeah, I'm magic, Mike. Just getting old I think!"

They all looked rinsed out to some degree. Apart from the natural variety on offer through either chamber porthole, more sporadic than weak, they hadn't been exposed to daylight for 12 days. The hours of sunlight had increased by another hour during their time above the site; the midnight sun would be pinned in the sky within two months. Not one single ray of which would ever reach down to the depth of *The Perseverance*.

A brief contract when compared to most jobs in the North Sea, which were measured more in weeks. All their diving equipment, suits and boots, helmets and gloves, looked the same as when they had set off. The only signs of wear and tear were frayed fibres of the regular rounds of gaffer tape dotted along the umbilicals, used to join the separate elements into a single hose. Though underneath the clothes, they all carried working injuries of one form or another. Roy, the one who had so nearly succumbed to the greatest injury, seemed least affected of all. He was left with only chest bruising, and could dive, or streak, again at a moment's notice. Brian still was limping slightly from an aubergine and ash grey haematoma that had drained from his ankle into the arch of his foot. Tim's neck was still in pain from resisting the violent attentions of the monkfish and Michael's back and right ribs were laid with small fluid blisters. He said it had felt like his back was being boiled after being scalded by too fierce a feed of hot water into his suit. Vitamin D was in short supply; when they took their first steps out on deck, they would be bleached enough to make the Peterheed locals appear olive-skinned and sun-kissed in comparison. Even on a relatively short stint in saturation, the effects of working in an invisible, dense custard and the inability to replenish the energy sapped from each dive were tolling. Following two years of inactivity, Brian had been the least prepared for the demands of the work.

Though the disparate divers would fill their time with further games of Backgammon or Uckers, softcore pornography and endless tea poured from a calcified pot, the supervisors were still to complete their shifts, overseeing the divers safe passage to the surface. Having spent seven consecutive days above the wreck location, a Russian Navy cruiser arrived on the site four hours later. The only ship pinging on their swooping radar screen was *Galloper*. But they reported no suspicions after the captain identified the ship as a mere fishing vessel, in answer to forceful advances over the naval radio frequency. So Roy may have been right about his collared visitor during dive number six; the whale was working in cahoots with those on the far side of the Iron Curtain.

The decompression included a generous number of rest stops, at Brian's insistence; they were scheduled to arrive at a single atmosphere two days after arriving back in Peterheed. With each day and the simulated pressure slowly reducing in the dive system, the four divers were raised 100 feet up in equivalent depth. But the storm front was beginning to envelope them, the winds that shrieked around the exterior were heard inside the chamber as were the waves that smashed over it. This burdened Brian with another element of buried concern. If the ship went down in the storm, there was no similarly pressurized lifeboat they could transfer into, until they were rescued. If *Galloper* was lost at sea, so would they be. The only role for the salvaged gold in that instance would be that it would pull the ship under just a little bit faster. The vessel was beginning to pitch and toss on an unseen sea inside their living chamber. Fragments of pack ice were crashing into the hull. Tables and chairs were sliding this way and that across the floor of *Galloper's* canteen with increasing momentum. The only items not fixed down in the chamber, were the decompressing divers and their possessions, which were prematurely packed into their luggage as they braced for a wild couple of days' passage. Davide confirmed as much, with his bloodless knuckles gripped tight against the edge of the dive panel.

"*Ze* storm will force us closer to *ze* shore. So we will be back in *Peter'ead* a day or two later, we *zink*. So you all should '*ave* a chance to," Davide sarcastically cleared his throat, "go and say '*ello* to Sergio in his cabin, before we '*and* '*im* over to *ze* Police." His four divers agreed that was a wonderful, deserving suggestion.

A delayed return to shore had no impact on the set length of decompression. The storm gave them something to pass the tedium that bit quicker, even if it was terrifying at times and impossible to sleep. The food passed through the service airlock, at great personal risk to the pot-smoking butler, switched to solids only. Boiled potatoes and meats. No soup and sauces. The storm also kept any prying eyes of an idle crew off the decks as they were confined to their cabins. The divers took all this in their restricted stride while they hunkered around the table drinking their tea and eating their meals. The time passed as quickly as the subjects they discussed. VHS or Betamax? Their deepest dive? Cassette or Compact Disc? Longest time spent in saturation? Favourite page three girl? Weirdest diving colleague?

Brian romped home with the prize on the latter subject, regaling stories of an eccentric German diver he had worked with in Borneo in 1974, aboard a barge named the *Benbecula*. Named Gunther Lehr, a flared-trousered former Hitler Youth conscript, when not saturation diving in the tropics, could be found travelling through South America on donkeyback, trading his diving dollars for gems and other precious stones as he meandered. Tim took the silver medal telling stories of an insanely intense ex-navy seal, who would dwell in saturation chambers for months at a time. His only indicator that it was time to decompress came when werewolves began to appear in the wet room mirror behind him as he shaved, in all too visceral hallucinations. Tim's lucid description rang bells for Michael, who suspected he might have spent a shift in the company of the same blood-shot-eyed lunatic. Roy was just happy he hadn't encountered any wolf eels on the wreck, "Bloody things, heads like granite footballs. They used to sit under the live pipelines in the North Sea, because of the warmth of the oil. When we used to have to sandbag the pipes, I always used my feet to push them in."

Michael had gathered a few artefacts from the wreck that he would claim as trophies. "I picked up a plate embossed with the name of the ship and a watch and chain. Having dived it now, I'm keen to find out more about this wreck when I get back."

At a virtual depth of 600 feet below sea level inside the walls of the chamber, Tim raised a topic they had all mused over once their plans were complete. What to do with the money? He highlighted the word "share" to mean more the contractual no-cure-no-pay percentage, with a face-bending wink: "So what's everyone's plan for their share?"

Before answering, Brian pointed up approximately to the vicinity of the diving bell where the concealed "share" sat and nodded, which Tim returned. Brian said, "Well, I'm meant to be getting married in Marseille later this year, so that will buy my beach bar in the south of France I reckon," Brian said as *Galloper* pounded through a wave with a structural crunch.

"Nice, brother. I'm heading down that way with my lady when we get back. Just get in the car and stop where the fuck we want on our way down."

Michael had his eye on a beachfront house in Great Yarmouth, which he could now afford to buy, with the leftover change funnelled into his idea of possibly opening a museum. Roy's desires were straightforward. He would buy a boat called "*Booze & Snooze*" to facilitate his search of the Plymouth seas. "My friend's getting rid. It's 21-foot-long and she's like a fat lady really. Sits well in the water. Good name too."

"Magic name. Well, you deserve it the most Roy, after what Sergio tried to pull on you," Brian said.

Tim agreed and provided further justification for their actions, "And that asshole, Bas. What a dumb, arrogant prick. If he's the best they can put forward as part of a consortium, what the fuck are the rest of 'em like? Man, he had one of those faces you just needed to smack, you know?"

Brian wasn't as inclined to violence as Tim, but even he had to concur that Bas's face would benefit from a fist punched into it. "You do have a point there, Tim." Roy seconded this with a naughty grin; Bas had clearly made a similar impression on all his divers. Michael concurred: "You're right there, matey. I wouldn't describe him as a charming man. Quite the opposite."

"Well, you never know, boys. If his papers aren't in order or the Ruskies find out about this, he'll probably end up getting jabbed with a poisoned umbrella by the KGB on a bridge in Amsterdam," Roy joked.

"Won't the locals want to board us on our way back, matey?" Michael asked, the thought had grown as Roy spoke.

"Nah, man. As long as the Norwegian authorities have some paperwork registered for the boat, they won't give a fucking toss." Tim had spent almost all of his diving life based out of Stavanger, so knew what he was talking about.

"I bet the *baastard* ain't too happy he didn't get all the gold out," Brian added, with some devilish pride.

"Oh, my heart fucking bleeds. He wouldn't have the balls to go and get it himself. I don't give a shit about a fucking arse end like that. I think he had more spray in his fucking hair when I met him than Joan fucking Collins," Tim observed without challenge.

Galloper saw out the storm on that rough return for two fraught days, then headed further offshore into open water in the Norwegian Sea, to the west of Norway. During that time, the simulated depth inside the chamber reduced by another 200 feet. A further 400 remained between them and freedom, along with retribution. Brian could almost taste his first cognac. The crew returned to loiter on the deck, carrying out simple tasks or staring over the sides of the ship for any first glimpses of land. Inside the chamber, they were intensely conscious of any movement or attention that might be drawn to the area on the dive system where the gold was concealed. Through a circular metal door hatch four divers would soon emerge, battered, bruised and short of time to tick off the steps that were needed to get their own gold ashore, before any police boarded the ship to arrest Sergio. That was not to mention dispatching their appointed Minister for Violence, Tim, to Sergio's cabin for a sustained and thorough pre-arrest beating. Until that moment, their lives still remained in the capable hands of Gordon and Davide. Brian's game of roulette with his own mortality would keep running for the duration, with the dancing ivory ball spinning for days before it came to rest in a coloured, numbered pocket.

Each had the experienced eye to routinely check themselves and their fellow divers for symptoms of decompression sickness. Four seasoned professionals would contend with frequent muscle and joint aches. This was so common that one was barely perceptible from the other in most cases. The onset of soreness associated with overuse injuries to the myofibrils of their depleted muscles could be felt for the first few days of decompression. Thereafter, most discomfort in the major joints was most likely to be caused by physiological responses to pressure changes on the lubricating synovial sacks that surrounded them.

They had all experienced less harmonious teams, with feuds and tension that simmered in the chamber, settled in the bars surrounding whichever port they docked at. Yet Tim, Roy, Michael and Brian had been a harmonious hyperbaric clan since first crossing swords in the hotel bar, before that night of chaos in the town of Peterhead. By the time the four remaining days of decompression were up, having turned the chamber into a cauldron of conniving, the crazy plot was clear to progress. There was no reason why they wouldn't operate as seamlessly as they had under the water. Roles were defined and agreed, as were approximate timings and Brian had volunteered to transport the gold back onto dry land, 42 years and one month after it had gone down with *The Perseverance*.

23. Peterhead Plunge

Four pairs of expectant eyes keenly watched as the circular handle of the main hatch door into the chamber spun anti-clockwise. It moved slowly at first while the threads were loaded, until it turned as freely as a bicycle wheel. The seal broke and the door audibly breathed as it swung open. On first inhalations of normal everyday air, the effects of helium immediately began to dissipate. Having acclimatised to the heightened pitch of their own voices while in saturation, a return to normal vocal frequency made each sound like a Barry White baritone to their own distorted ears. One by one, each diver stepped out of the inert chamber into a cacophony of foul everyday smells: diesel, cigarette smoke or the bitter grease smeared over ferrous deck mountings. They walked straight into the substantial arms of Captain Shenchenko. Enamoured by the impending payday for a short charter, in turn he embraced Michael, Roy, Tim and Brian in a cheap cologne and rum-laced bear-hug so tight, it nearly winded them all. Each surreptitiously checked the end capping was still sound and had not been tampered with, as they swayed around in the Skipper's joyous clutches.

"You're like John Wayne, boom boom, cowboy, yes?!" was Captain Shenchenko's way of extolling his gratitude for the results of their wild bravery, as he released Brian. His crew joined Davide and Gordon to shape an irregular semi-circle on the lit deck around the chamber exit for a concluding polaroid picture. Lots of back-patting and instinctive applause broke out, as if they were welcoming home four astronauts to Earth. They were indeed returning from the alien world of inner space, where less was known to science than the surfaces of distant planets. Even at six in the morning, there was no less fascination among the crew in the endurance and monastic sacrifice the four residents of the chamber had demonstrated. With reluctance visible in both his manner and tone, Davide stepped forward to explain he had been asked by Bas to search the divers – a surprise they had all seen coming.

"Bas is not '*appy* about *ze* missing four bars. '*E zinks* you '*ave zem*. So I '*ave* to search you one by one as you exit. Please don't be offended by *zis*?" Davide informed them, sheepishly. But the search was so rudimentary, it was as non-offensive as it was comical. Clearly going through the motions, he briefly moved their soiled clothes and personal possessions around inside each bag.

"No hard feelings, Dave. You can search in the pot too if you want," Brian said as his bag was momentarily rummaged through, more for effect on the surrounding watchers, as Davide was much better informed. Normal practice would see the divers clearing out the chamber, in readiness for a diving crew change. The beds would be stripped, floors swept and dirty linen handed to the diving tenders, no longer through the service hatch. But this was a one-off job. The dive system that had maintained them at pressure would be lifted off the deck to God knows where next. This would be closely followed by purging the hull of its helium and oxygen cylinders, spent or otherwise.

The twinkling lights of Peterhead and its surrounds were fading out in the dawn; the wider Aberdeenshire scenery was still to be revealed in the lingering darkness overhead. Light drizzle, more like fine mist spores, was blown in the wind across the bow of *Galloper*, and the deck lights illuminated the coastal waters of the North Sea as they slipped past the side of the hull. Davide pivoted himself away from the group and dipped his shoulder to mutter in Brian's ear, hypothetical words that would be lost in the noise of the crew.

"If I were you and if I '*ad ze* gold, I would get it off *ze* ship if you can before we dock in *ze 'arbour. Ze* police will be taking Sergio in. So I would say you '*ave* about an '*our* to get yourself organised."

"OK. Magic. I need a favour first, though. Can you let me see Sergio quickly before I take care of other business?"

"Ah, of course. I nearly forget *zis*," Davide said; each of his replies were spoken close to Brian's ear.

"I just want to check if it's who I think it is, Dave?"

"Ah, yes. *Zis* Raynor chap you told me about?"

"Yep. Then Tim can go pay him a proper visit after."

A pact unsaid, telegraphed in a wink, saw them pause for ten minutes, mainly for the crew to be drawn away off the deck by the weather, so they would be within earshot of Tim's impending explosion. Davide flicked his head over his left shoulder, gesturing for Brian to follow him. Brian read this and repeated the gesture to Tim while shouting his name to gain his attention. Brian and Tim followed Davide through to Sergio's locked cabin, over the lipped doorways and stooping beneath ducting.

"Wait here a second," Brian asked of Tim, ten feet short of the cabin door in which Davide was turning a key in the lock.

Inside, through a partially open door was a disorientated Sergio in a velour dressing gown, having been woken in the pre-morning by his lock snapping open. As Sergio reached from the bunk for his half rim spectacles with his hands and slippers with his feet, Brian recognised him immediately. Sergio, as he had been called on the *Galloper*, was Charles Raynor as Brian unfortunately had known him. Brian simply pulled the door closed and spoke as he walked along the dim corridor they had entered the structure through.

"Yeah, that's him. Fire away Tim. For Roy. And me and Malcom too please."

Brian traded places in the narrow corridor where Tim had been waiting and watched as his irate colleague pushed Charles's door wide open and grinned as he announced, "I've come to give you Roy's share, you motherfucker."

Tim was off the leash, released from his cylindrical home and ready to square up to his ex-supervisor. He had volunteered for the task of remonstrating with Charles in a most physical manner on behalf of his colleagues – it was very much his forte. With great menace, Tim stepped slowly and silently in. Before the door was slammed shut and locked behind him, Brian heard Charles trying to reason with an unannounced visitor he recognised by his Canadian accent.

"Hey, let's be reasonable about this. I kept my mouth shut, buddy," Charles howled, in an ever rising tone like that of a filling bottle, crowning the absurdity of any remaining claim he might later make to his stake. The crashes and bangs, slams and thumps, screams and cries of Charles being knocked around his cabin slowly lured the inquisitive crew into the corridor, like moths to a candle. This had the secondary benefit of keeping their attention away from the rear deck, where Brian was headed. Their final act as a diving team was to get Brian off the stern of the ship, as close into the harbour as they dared, with as few eyes noticing as possible. This all had the extra element of tension, as he knew the police would be boarding the ship when it came to dock – not something that was alien to Brian.

Michael acted as a watchman of sorts, loitering between the dive shack and empty chamber entrance, with clear sight of the superstructure and exits onto the deck. Roy moved the diving equipment to the very end of the stern as Brian climbed up the chamber, using the netting for hand and footholds. He wedged his knee under the end cap before beginning to remove the retaining wire. One by one, he quickly passed the four glinting bars over his contorted midriff and dropped them onto the empty deck, each making a satisfying soft thump as it landed. To cover their tracks somewhat, Brian swiftly re-seated the end capping in place while moving himself back off the system.

The collars of Roy's orange overalls fluttered in the breeze, as he stood next to a single dry suit, folded down in such a way that Brian could just step into it and Roy could swiftly assist with dressing him in. Beside the dry suit was a body harness with a single scuba bottle and bailout attached. Roy had already hooked this up to the Bellman's band-mask. Already dressed in a shirt, tie, sweater, trousers and his cocoa brown leather jacket beneath his under-suit, with his Italian shoes, he stepped into the dry suit. Roy immediately pulled the suit up as Brian thrust both hands down through the sleeves and out of the cuffs. A couple of shoulder rolls settled the outer dry-suit on his torso before the zip was fastened shut. Down came the band-mask over his head and the hasty fitting soon followed. Roy's last act as dive support was sliding gold bars into the sides of the wellington boots Brian just trod in. A pair of bars in either boot were swiftly sealed with rings of gaffer tape wrapped about his shins.

Having surveyed the scene and task facing Brian, Roy tapped his approval on Brian's shoulder, before adding dryly, "Rather you than me, *Broin*! You must be nuts!" Now free of duties and intrigued by Brian's mettle, Roy and Michael paired up and spoke their matching incredulous thought in unison. Brian's willingness to see out his part of the scheme without hesitation or delay beggared belief.

"What the fuck is he doing?"

They had a point. Brian had only just made it out alive of decompression. That had been his largest, lingering fear from the start of their press down. Now he was waiting to time his jump off the back of the ship as his corner of the deck eased over closest to the passing water with a hundred weight of bullion in his wellington boots. He had no local knowledge of tides or currents. He couldn't know whether they would simply spit him back out into the open North Sea. The depth was an uneducated guess; his only guide was the mass of the ships able to access the port. Semi-submersible rigs dotted along the greater coastline were a less encouraging indication of his impending drop. To Brian's left, a tantalising gap of only 50 feet off starboard side to land lay between him and the valuable benefits he would reap if he were to make it safely.

Brian watched the bubbling foam drift back away from the stern, two feet below his gold weighted boots. The horizon was a few shades lighter back out to sea in the east than behind him to the west. Illuminated boats and ships of all shapes and sizes were on the same heading as *Galloper*, making it seem a disorganised sprint for home. Brian waited to catch a sight of the row of giraffe-like cranes along Albert Quay and feel the ensuing turn to starboard around the tip of the breakwater before he leapt off, pin-jumping through the fizzing wake. He had both hands pushing down on his band-mask, so the upward force of the water striking the chin couldn't remove his well-arranged teeth, or break his jaw entirely.

In the faint, drizzly light with Brian barely just a sole silhouette, they watched his right arm reach up to twist his air valve open on his mask. The next second, Brian and his big-budget version of concrete boots were gone.

Roy spun around to gauge whether Brian's leap off the ship had gone unseen. He kept at least one monitoring eye fixed on their nearest point under the small breakwater lighthouse while making slow, meandering steps toward the stern. Their salvage voyage was minutes from ending; all involved would soon be making merry in the nearest bar, hopefully. The shanty Roy had sung on leaving the same port had brought him the most fortune of all. He buckled one knee forward, stooping to lean on *Galloper's* rails and found himself quietly repeating the salty verse, not to bolster any of his own good luck, but because he felt *Broin* might need it.

> *We'll be back to port soon to see my Sally*
>
> *Away to sea we must go*
>
> *Open the sails, man the rudder*
>
> *We are headed to Plymouth Hoe*
>
> *Well, pour another rum, Jack*
>
> *Let those currents be true,*
>
> *Fill the sails with your best, and...*
>
> *Bring us back to shore... Broin.*

24. Golden Hour

The few fishing smacks moored nearby still pursued a living from the sea, rather than being converted to supply vessels for the offshore industry. That morning's haul of haddock was being slowly hoisted ashore in woven baskets. The air above each vessel was thick with hooting gulls as personnel in yellow dungarees processed and packaged the catch, ready for market. On the opposite side of the basin, masked welders flickered in turquoise light as they showered molten sparks from running repairs to oil drilling, surveying or rig-tugging vessels. Rain or shine, and in gales or storms, the works continued ceaselessly, day and night.

The fall of Scottish rain intensified soon after Brian disappeared under the water, tamping down the gentle harbour swell, as *Galloper* manoeuvred into its bay. A brace of crew threw mooring ropes onto the quay from either end of the ship. An anonymous black van, windowless apart from the cabin, was parked next to a Ford Granada in police colours. A carrot orange sash ran the length of both sides of the vehicle; edging the stripe was a reflective blue tape. Over which the words 'Grampian Police' were displayed on both front doors. The crew and diving team would prove too canny a clan for this constabulary, whose beat officers were in attendance to take Charles into custody. The officers weren't to know the twenty-eight gold bars would eventually be moved into the blacked-out, waiting van. The four others were strapped to Brian's ankles as he toiled across the bowels of the harbour.

While *Galloper* was elegantly positioned by Captain Shenchenko, Brian's progress was anything but serene. For balance and impact protection, Brian had spread all his limbs out around him as he dropped through the water. His undeclared cargo, pulling him down through the icy, mute darkness, was reducing his estimates at depth to guesswork. The only soundtrack was the slightly panicked rush and whoosh of each breath beneath the many ships thundering above his head. Looser panels of his dry suit flapped like a raincoat in a hilltop storm as he dropped. The jolting cold registered first by seeping through his gloves. Every joint, be it his wrists or ankles were aching before he landed on an algae trimmed anchor chain. Without any idea to what degree he had rotated during the descent, he spun the valve on his bailout to fill his suit with gas and left it open. Obeying gravity, the gas accumulated in the top half of his suit, giving him the appearance of a waterborne American Football player. The bulges and pockets of air were squeezed through seams and joints in bubbles and gulps as he manoeuvred himself to his left. The buoyancy idea Roy had devised of hooking the bailout cylinder onto where the missing hot water supply would ordinarily connect, appeared to be working. Brian wasn't buoyant in the classical sense, by any means. His boots were still firmly planted in the yielding mud of the harbour floor. However awkward it was to shift his arms and torso in the semi-inflated suit, it did lighten his movements. The air was providing partial support in the unlikely form of a diver-shaped lift-bag.

Brian guessed he only had to swim, scramble, slip, swear, slide and step his way 50 feet to his starboard side, and if he made it that far on a questionable bearing, he had to find a concealed route up onto the breakwater. Through a slow, forceful current, breathing air from his tank and haemorrhaging bailout heliox through his suit, he advanced up the nearest rise of the harbour bed. Blind, with no torch and none of the usual communications with topside, he was completely cut off and unaided. He was alone on an insane dive that none of his fellow divers, supervisors or crew, would, or could admit knowledge of. It was a public inquest just waiting to happen, if the wrong route were taken. He was guided only by the information being pawed to his brain, through chilled wrists, aching hands and numb fingers. Every next move was dictated by the highest point in reach. His persistence finally paid off as he felt a welcome sandy crunch above his cranium. He had head butted a single boulder, part of a thick seam of rock armour protecting the base of the structure. Lifting his head brought his faceplate above the water and the delights of Peterhead back into view. The canopy of clouds had become lighter in shade since Brian leapt off *Galloper*.

"*Baastard*!" Brian mused to himself, with palpable relief as he searched for a route up.

As he pulled himself out of the water, the amplified levels of gravity loaded up Brian's boots for the climb. Just below the brow of the breakwater, invisible from the feeder road below that ran the entirety of the embankment, he began to remove his diving equipment. The dry suit wasn't his so could be tossed back into the sea. The same went for the under-suit, his harness and spent cylinders attached; he aimed the latter at his floating suits, to take them all down to the bottom. All he needed to keep was his wellington boots and his band-mask. The rain bounced from the shoulders of his leather jacket as he pulled the zip up to his Adam's apple. All the clothes he was wearing below the under-suit were already saturated to touch, but his head looked remarkably dry in comparison. This gave more of an impression of someone just arriving for work, rather than signing off from what had become a potentially lethal salvage project. Brian brushed his wild black locks over his right eyebrow to reinstate a measure of a parting and scratched his fingertips through his moustache before leaning down to collect his kit.

His inauspicious entry into the industry had been 15 years earlier, below the docks of London. He was emerging from similar surroundings, but in much more advanced equipment, and significantly wealthier. He no longer had the spherical brass dome helmet with portholes, chest weights and lead-lined boots of the "standard dress". Just the Bellman's band-mask swinging from his left hand and his boots, as he traversed the concrete steps down onto the road. To Brian's relief, *Galloper* was not immediately in sight. He had a rare few minutes of peace with himself to fully appreciate the outcome of their plan. He wandered deeper into the port, aiming for a large car park marking a kink in the supply road. It was the kind of car park Brian had abandoned his old Maserati Merak in many times. It was in front of a glazed terminal from which he had used to take his helicopter flights out to the oil-rigs dotting the North Sea. There were scarlet Ferraris, winged Lamborghinis and Porsche 911s. Auto exotica lingering under a layer of encrusted salt, in the most prosaic port setting. Of the three Porsches, only one was the black 928, registered with a new B number plate that Brian had ordered in Brighton. He leant down to run his hand over the wet tread of the rear tyre on the passenger side, his palm still caked with damp grit having already searched the driver's side. With feeling gradually returning in his fingers and as arranged, he emerged clutching a set of two keys, each with a dimpled plastic head and slender notched blade. This soon opened the door on the same side so he could store his heavy boots and wet mask in the foot well. The smell of freshly moulded plastic and tanning of the tobacco leather seats was cut off when he slammed the door shut. It was a luxurious invasion through the sinuses, replacing the usual feed of salty diesel aromas, with a hint of rotten fish found in harbours. It was an irresistible scent to the likes of Tim, Michael, Roy and Brian, nonetheless.

From where Brian stood shivering in the car park, the green bow of *Galloper* was just in sight; he knew he and his co-divers might be in the clear. It was 7°C, barely double the temperature of the water from which Brian had just emerged. The rain reverted to drizzle as he walked briskly back to the ship. He acted as "natural" as he could, periodically blowing his breath into his cupped hands, trying to warm himself further.

"*Aye*, where did *ye* spring from, laddy?" asked one rust-haired police officer, emitting a cloud of coarse condensation. He was standing by the gangplank leaning on *Galloper*. His peaked cap displayed the same chequered band as his English counterparts.

Brian gave a winning smile and explained to the policeman, "I didn't spring from anywhere. I'm working on this boat."

"I did *ne* see *ye* walk off the *boot*?" the officer probed curtly.

"That doesn't mean I'm not working on it, does it? I'm one of the divers."

The officer's stare narrowed with an air of doubt. He critically surveyed this man who, rather than modelling the typical grizzled seafarer look, looked more like he had just stepped out of an all-night casino. In a sense, Brian just had. And he had sufficient winnings in his footwell to forge Anne an engagement ring the size of a doughnut. Before the bamboozled officer had time to respond, Brian backed his claim up by waving at Roy, who was still resting on the ship railings. "You alright, Roy?"

"Yeah, *Broin*. We've gotta make statements or something," Roy shouted back.

Brian's obvious familiarity with his colleagues and ship's crew overrode any misgivings the officer had about his story. Mindful he was in attendance because of graver matters, the officer let Brian pass, to re-board *Galloper*. He slowly dried himself out in the canteen while waiting to provide a witness statement, to support the charges of attempted murder against Charles. Soon after, the offending ex-supervisor was marched off the ship in handcuffs into the waiting car. Tim's handiwork was much in evidence as Charles limped, winced and groaned his way onto the back seat. His face was covered in grazes, bruises and inflammation. He was insisting repeatedly for all to hear that he had been working on a gold salvage job and the divers had pilfered four bars of gold for themselves.

To extinguish any embers of doubt, Brian offered confidently, "You're welcome to search us and the dive system if you don't believe us." To which all his colleagues solemnly nodded agreement. Gordon was less aware of the goings-on than Davide, but had just enough skin in the game; he didn't want the "official" concealed gold walk off the ship with the police. As dive superintendent, he pooh-poohed Charles's notion as much as the rest, calling it laughable to suggest they had been doing anything other than pipeline inspections.

"*Ney* bother," was the judgement of Charles's arresting officer to these accusations. "And don't *ye* worry *aboot* how he looks too. Between us, we'll say he fell *doon* a *wee* set of stairs in the station!"

One by one, with their recollection of events recorded, the diving team were released from *Galloper*. Waiting for each other on the quayside, with the realisation of what they appeared to have pulled off dawning, an insatiable thirst developed to go and celebrate in local taverns. Gordon had dutifully volunteered to give his statement last, so as not to detain his divers any longer than necessary. So Davide was the second last to leave the ship. He joined the loitering divers on the quayside. Inside his holdall was his collection of frogs, cleared out of the dive shack. Rolled up on top of Roy's luggage was his polar bear skin, tied with a belt of a dressing gown. Michael was well turned out and back in good spirits, all his wreck research material had received little attention during an overly anxious stay in compressed isolation. And Tim was clearly just itching to get to the nearest watering hole. His patience for alcoholic abstinence had completely run out. Charles remained in the police car until the second officer was finished with Gordon.

"So, we must do *zis* again sometime, gentlemen?" Davide announced as he lit a slim Panatella cigar.

"I could be tempted, Dave?" Brian replied, as a smile grew. "Where are we off to next then?"

"You never know. It '*as* been a real pleasure working *wiz* you all. I '*ave* a plane to catch boys, but promise me *somezing*?"

"What's that, Dave?" Michael asked for the group.

"Be careful none of you injure yourselves falling off your wallets, ok?"

As he had a pressing meeting to arrange with Christian on a south coast pier of his choosing, Brian chose not to join the revelry. All hands were warmly shaken, phone numbers and addresses exchanged with invites to visit each other. He also had a new car to enjoy, a new toy to add to the long list he had owned throughout his life. The door closed with a mechanical clunk as he settled into the leather bucket seats. The rev-counter-dominated instrument cluster was alien to his eye. The oil pressure gauge and brake failure warning light warranted almost constant attention in his Maserati, something he hoped to avoid with more everyday Germanic engineering. This had been paid for by the secrets the wreck of the *Dalhousie* had given up and earned by much endeavour, acting on the research he had done on dry land. He turned the ignition key in the steering column to fire the engine under the long bonnet in front of him. A muffled growl emanated, following a touch of the accelerator. The Blaupunkt stereo pushed out a pearlescent compact disc from its bay, by a group or singer he hadn't heard of named "Sade".

Brian sat there lighting a cigarette, as he waited for his new engine to warm up. The fruits of an industry he found impossible to say no to were self-evident. For all the fears he had carried into the chamber before the press down, throughout the job and especially during the decompression, he had survived it. He was a man with an innate capacity for danger or adventure, to whom the normal or average was stifling. Would he agree to a similar project were it offered in his future? He would probably give it serious consideration. Just as long as his doctor or mother didn't find out. His journey back to Brighton began with him following the feeder road out of the docks and back past *Galloper* one last time. His colleagues were yet to vacate the moss-tinged cobbles on which they chatted and where Charles was still held in the police car, so Brian pulled up beside them and lowered the electric window.

"Speak to you soon guys. Magic," Brian said, taking a hand off the steering wheel and poked a thumb high out of the window. To have sloped off quietly in such circumstances, in powerful German machinery, would only have aroused suspicions in their story. Normal behaviour for returning offshore workers would be to build up the engine to four thousand revs before dropping the clutch into first gear. Next would be to exit the scene with great swagger in a customary cloud of choking rubber smoke. So, to stay in character, that's exactly what Brian did for the benefit and entertainment of his workmates.

Epilogue

On leaving the docks, and passing through the booms and security booths, he pushed the compact disc back into the music system. His attention merged with the engine noise, as he grew accustomed to his shiny new toy, following the road signage through hamlet and village for the route south-west to Aberdeen. Drops of rain pinged against the windscreen before the wipers dragged the spring shower aside. Something he had overlooked when buying the new car in the showroom was the amount of glass on the rear end. A long glazed boot lid between two curving quarter-lights, a third of the overall length, meant he had plunged an awful lot of money into a car that was one third greenhouse, clearly not designed for life in Southern Europe.

The liquid crystal display of the car phone handset, mounted to the passenger side of the central console level with the gear stick, shone lime green. On his first stretch of clear, straight road, he unclipped it and dialled Anne's number with the rubberised buttons. To his delight, it began to ring in his ear. A split second before her answer machine cut in on the fourth ring, she answered.

"*Allo?*"

"Morning. It's Brian."

What reached Anne's ear was a robotic version of her intended. "*Bri-yon, Fantastique!* You are OK? *Everyzing* OK?" she asked excitedly.

"Either my doctor is wrong or I just got lucky, but I'm fine! No aches or pains apart from the usual. Well my ankle is sore but that's about it. We got back a few hours ago. I'm heading back to Brighton now. Sorry I couldn't phone you from the boat, darlin',"

"Ahh, no problem."

"I'm phoning from my new car, don't you know."

"*Ze* new car? Fancy! As long as I know you're fine, *zen* I can relax."

"I'll survive. Did pretty well out of it too," Brian said, while looking down towards the proceeds planted in the footwell. "I have something to take care of back in Brighton first, then I'll head down to you. Shouldn't be longer than a week. I'll get the hovercraft over from Portsmouth."

"OK. My cousin Lolly '*as* been trying to get in touch *wiz* you too. '*E* says '*e* carried on with some research. '*E* '*as zis* idea *zat zere* was *anozer* wreck on top, or just to *ze* side of *ze Dalhousie* that '*as* platinum on it.? Called *ze Rivonia*, so '*e* says. Or *some'zing* like *zis*."

"Mmm, that sounds interesting," he replied, although he was certain that the platinum wasn't on the wreck of the *Rivonia* anymore, no matter how fastidious Lolly's research had been. But it did mean that the unknown cargo of the *Dalhousie* that had so intrigued Brian and Lolly was probably still down there. The only mention of it had been a figure of £100,000 denoted on the East Indiaman's incomplete inventory in 1853 – a value of £1.5

million, 132 years later, "He's been keeping busy! I'll give him a call when I'm back home later."

"OK, can't wait to see you. Are you sure you're OK to drive all *zat* way?"

"Yeah, I'll be fine in a few days' time. I should get my share paid out in a week or two."

"Great! And all *ze* guys you were working *wiz* OK?

"Yeah no problems, Anne. We're all good as gold."

DEDICATION

Georges Arnoux was a key player in improving the safety of North Sea diving operations in the pioneer days. A benefit of this is many people still are alive today, who otherwise wouldn't be with us.

I arrived at Montpellier airport on a Friday evening in Nov 2017, en route to meet him for the first time. He was dispatched as proxy to collect me by his wife, Anne, who had known Brian for 40 years and was most insistent I come for a visit. Not knowing what Georges looked like among the collection of rare characters leaning against the short arrivals barrier, I phoned the number Anne had furnished, while scanning the line to see who answered. A man with thick, parted grey hair and narrow eyes pulled a ringing phone from his jacket pocket. His lip movements matched the voice in my ear and that is how I first met him. We drove back to his and Anne's house in partnership, as Georges had forgotten his glasses – I read the road signs while he took the correct turnoff.

Three enjoyable days passed on my first visit with Anne & Georges; he was initially unaware I was the nephew of one of the divers he would have been responsible for. He drew sketch after sketch, fed me rum upon exotic rum, and showed me graphs and charts, all the while educating me in the fascinating and lethal era of commercial diving. I had no intention of writing Salvamar before that serendipitous visit, but George and Anne changed that:

George with his knowledge and Anne with the cache of stories and some 30 letters Brian had sent to her over 40 years.

On a following visit with Brian's sister (my mother), he raised English bunting up his driveway flagpole prior to opening a bottle of champagne with a sabre – a well-known party trick of his and quite the welcome for us. Due to COVID restricting movements over the last two years, I never got to thank Georges in person for all the time and effort he took in making me understand the subject as well as I could. And a few of the stories he shared across that kitchen table are in this book.

So R.I.P. Georges... and thank you so much for your abundant knowledge, enthusiasm and Anglo-Gallic wit.

While good people can enhance your life, special ones can change it.

Also available from the same author

Long Walk For Nothing (Amazon-2016) – An account of his 765 km fundraising walk across South Africa in an ostrich costume.

Comper – The Novel (Amazon-2017) – A professional competition enterer uncovers the self-suicide plot of a South African mining magnate.

Category D (Amazon-2018) – A prison-break novel from a British open prison.

Salvamar – A Tale of Salvage & Deep Diving (Amazon-2019) – A biographical novel about the eventful life and times of a North Sea pioneering diver.